THE SHINING SERPENT

EMAY AMORE

Twin
Rivers

The Shining Serpent

A catalogue record for this book is available from the British Library.

ISBN 978-0-9573311-1-2

Published by Twin Rivers Limited

For more copies of this book, please email:
info@theshiningserpent.co.uk

Website: http://www.emayamore.com

Designed and Set by Twin Rivers Limited

Printed in Great Britain.

"Only when you drink from the river
of silence shall you indeed sing"
- Kahlil Gibran

THE SHINING SERPENT

Chapter 1

The Eclipse

The smoke and dust rose to the skies vivifying the chaos and destruction, and like a demon intruding upon the earth, they shaded the world in darkness. Explosions sent shattered glass flying and raining down to the ground. The flames glazed the vicinity, and the bodies lay scattered among the soporific winds. The screams were digging into her very being, leaving her glancing at the wall in fear. She closed her eyes, hoping never to wake, hoping never to see what lay beneath the dark veil of the night. But the nights in Iraq were dark, cold, yet never silent.

The next day she awoke dazed, a dull pain spread through her skull and spine. The sunlight crept through the window warming her wrinkly flesh. She tried to resist, she tried to return to her peaceful slumber, but she couldn't. Digging her elbows into the mattress and barely able to sustain her weight, she rose. She was old, frail and weak. Yet she had something that kept her strong through all the chaos; her one and only son. She was a woman living in Iraq, her name was Sarah.

She clawed her way into the bathroom, struggling to reach the sink. Washing her face, she felt her hard tough hands tug her wrinkly flesh with each stroke. Staring into the mirror, she once again asked herself, where did the years go? From flying kites in the sunny skies of Baghdad, to dodging bombs and bullets. She had forgotten her childhood, to her, it was a mere illusion, an old dream that she can scarcely remember. Wiping these thoughts from her mind she rushed to the kitchen to make breakfast for her young son Ali.

Sectarian violence had dramatically increased in the past few years, and as she cooked breakfast, she remembered all the friends she lost, not only in the diaspora, but also those caught in the crossfire. The majority of the middle class families had left, and like a swarm of gazelle fleeing a beast, they did not look back. She wasn't angry at them though, she knew that if she had enough money, she would have done the same. She took a moment, sighing as she fantasized about the west. A place where people told her was like a living paradise. It was a place she had heard where even a dog has rights.

She lived in a small house and made ends meet by baking pastries. Her husband's death was unexpected to say the least; he died of cancer the previous year. They thought he was cured, they thought the treatment went well, but it simply lay dormant until it struck again. The last thing he saw, was his wife rush towards him as he fell. Her hugs weren't enough, and he drew his last breath looking into her eyes. At least he spent the last few days of his life happy, she thought to herself. He spent his last hours in this world with his family.

Her mind wandered once again, and just as quick as she had enjoyed her reminiscence, she was now thinking of the previous night. The sound of the bullets that whizzed by her house tormented her. Like a fiend usurping her thoughts, she couldn't stop thinking about them, and like the sound of the explosions, these thoughts reverberated in her mind. Yet these images that haunted her so vehemently were not the worst; it was seeing the piled up bodies that made her cry. Bodies of young and old, male and female, all were piled atop each other as families wept, their voices filling the silence. And even though she could see the explosions and the destruction, those that were responsible could not be seen, and who they were, was unknown. No one knew, and yet everyone was angry. All were ready; weapons were held high, they spoiled for a fight. Men searched, looking for someone to blame, hoping that by doing so, that they may feel a little peace on the inside.

Shattered hearts ached with memories of loved ones, and as the devastated families wept and mourned, they would cry calling for intervention in God's name. Yet they were not alone, the criminals and murderers' voices echoed in the cold nights of Mesopotamia, committing their atrocities in the name of that same God.

Watching your neighbour's cadaver being dragged across the desert floor, and then piled upon a mass of rotting flesh made you stop and think. It made you question the government, it made you question the American forces, and most fervently did it make you question the humanity of your fellow man. To Sarah, morality became a subjective endeavour. That in this land, chaos and order could no longer be distinguished. The sound of weeping mothers plagued her mind. After feeding her son, she held him tightly, kissing his forehead.

Before long it was time to begin work; she had prepared the dough the night before, and so she began baking. And just as soon as she had started, she could hear her friend's voice calling her. It was Nadda, her childhood friend. Nadda was an interesting woman; she came from a rich family, yet surprisingly continued to live in the same house. She was also a Christian, yet she remained in Iraq. Their symbiotic relationship was sustained by their humble demeanour. Nadda came in through the front door, early, before any of the customers.

"How are you doing my dear friend," said Nadda softly as she embraced Sarah. "Here, let me help you," Nadda forcibly pushed her way across to knead more dough.

"Have you spoken to Noor? I haven't seen her in a long time," said Sarah.

"No I haven't, I keep asking and looking for her, but she's just disappeared," replied Nadda as she thrust her knuckles into the warm dough.

"What do you think happened to her?"

"Her house is empty... She probably left," reasoned Nadda.

"She left without saying goodbye?"

"That's what it looks like, she must have had her reasons. Maybe she found love, maybe she didn't have time to think."

"I saw that girl grow from a little child playing in the streets," Sarah whimpered back. A silence soon befell both of them as they continued their work. It was an awkward silence, one that could not be avoided, they just did not know what to say, they did not know what they should have been thinking at that point in time.

"We all need to stick together," said Sarah. Nadda remained silent as Sarah continued her little outburst. "If everyone were to stick together, if everyone were to be fearless, then Saddam would have never gained power."

The women worked in silence, lost in a sea of their own reminiscences. Occasionally they would speak of inequality; news of an insidious corruption within the Iraqi government had reached them, and so they spoke of the government officials, stolen money and attempted assassinations.

Little Ali was looking on at them from behind the door. They thought he was playing on his own in the other room, but Ali was getting bored, he wanted to play outside with other kids. The shimmering sun made the ground glimmer and was very appealing. Ali silently walked away from the two women as they toiled. He looked over his shoulder, smoothly weaving and turning from corner to corner like a small mouse. He reached for the front door, the sun's rays blinding his eyes as he reached for the door handle, it reminded him of the days when he could walk barefoot in the warm grass; a time where it was safe.

The memories played back in his mind, memories of when he used to climb the mulberry tree. Memories of chasing a butterfly as it fluttered up and beyond his reach; its wings decorated with vibrant crimson and dark green. He shook himself awake as he pulled on and twisted the door handle. However, before he could even open the door, he felt a sudden tug on his left shoulder. Something had grabbed him with force, pulling him away from the light, away from the freedom he sought. He gasped in fear.

"What have we told you about going outside," said Nadda as the child tried to ignore her. He knew about the dangers, he knew that there were kidnappers and murders. But he also knew about the feeling of a cold breeze on a sunny day, how it would send soothing waves of bliss with its tender touch.

As Nadda cautioned him, speaking of the dangers that lurked in the streets, in his mind he dreamt of freedom, and just as Nadda had finished her little speech, Ali went into the next room to play.

"I don't know what to do about that boy," said Sarah as she sighed.

"Boys always want to play outside."

"Nadda?" asked Sarah in a hushed voice.

"Yes?"

"Why do you stay here? You should go to a safer country. You are in a bigger danger than anyone else, and you have the money to leave. I know people who would leave at the first opportunity... But you stay?"

"Well... This is my home, I can't leave, I don't know how to, I can't imagine it. I can't imagine not waking up to my neighbourhood. We grew up together, we saw the rise and fall of our nation... And through it all, through the cold darkness, we kept each other warm."

"But why would you stay... Forget me. Go, just go and live your life."

"But this is my life; this is the only life I know. I can't do what the others do, not after what I've seen. I can't go and live a carefree life with a nice house in the west. I can't do that and pretend as if everything is fine. I've seen people do it, but I don't understand how they do it. I just don't... We have to unite, we are all one."

"Are we one? Are we really?" asked Sarah in sadness.

"We are all one, but we just don't realize it yet. There are good people in Iraq, the people that are willing to risk their lives, just to help others," said Nadda with conviction.

"Do you remember the days when life was easier?" asked Sarah.

"I can't seem to remember them."

"They were the days when electricity and water were easy to come by, the days when my husband had enough fuel to actually drive."

"It's not too bad," replied Nadda trying to stay optimistic. "Things will get better, and what we have now should suffice," at that moment the electricity stopped and the humming of the fan was no longer heard. The women looked around the room laughing.

"Okay, so it's not perfect," said Nadda in jest.

"What about the water?" asked Sarah.

"You've just got to learn to hurry up in the shower, and make sure to fill every bottle quick enough."

"What about petrol? People have to wait seven hours in a queue to get petrol these days," said Sarah.

"Then just dig a hole in the ground yourself, I'm sure you'll find something," the women laughed, making the most of what they had.

They spoke of their school days, for the present bore no fruit, and all they had, were their dreams, dreams of a normal and simple life. They had lived their childhood in mirth, and yet their children hadn't experienced the same. Their children never experienced running through the street with a kite in hand, hearing the soothing whistles of the wind. No, they were trapped inside their houses all day; watching their country ravished and destroyed from the inside. And even though the people were proud, they were subject to the decisions and whims of leaders; the politicians, the gangsters, the thieves, and the murderers.

Though Sarah and Nadda spoke scornfully of their miserable lives, and of their cherished past, they understood that others had it worse. They knew that there were orphans living in the streets, and they knew that they could not begin to understand what kind of trauma such young children could go through.

"Did you hear what happened earlier this week across the street?" asked Nadda.

"What happened?"

"A friend was walking back home, and as she walked, an American soldier appeared out of nowhere." Nadda stopped for a moment taking a breath. "He held a gun in his hand, and he took his gun, and put it between his own eyes. He looked straight at her, his eyes were red, his hands shaking, and his legs weak. He looked at her and apologized, he looked scared, mucus and tears covered his face. She couldn't understand what he was saying. She was so scared and shocked; she just looked at him stunned. He pulled his trigger... and, and," Nadda stopped.

"Why did he do that?" Sarah asked in shock.

"He had killed a child…"

"A child?"

"Yeah… The woman was questioned by the Americans a few days later, they told her that he had fired his gun earlier that day, and a stray bullet had killed someone."

"So why did he… in front of her?"

"Apparently, she looked like the child's mother; he thought that she was that mother." Sarah listened in shock. Stories from all around her neighbourhood had been circulating, but one so close to where they lived was rare. Normally, the stories they would hear would be about a massacre or something else of that nature, but never had they heard of a suicidal soldier. And with that Sarah comforted her friend, she did not have answers, but she listened, she was there; she was present in the dark moments of her life.

"I am haunted by that image, a man with a gun to his head. A foreigner lying in a pool of tears."

"Not all soldiers are bad," said Sarah.

"They kill," replied Nadda angrily, "No one should kill, not like this. Why are they even here?"

"Because they are the blind victims of injustice, they are tools, they are government dogs. The man that took his life, he has a mother, he was once a child."

"They should rebel!" said Nadda.

"Rebellion, revolution..." Sarah paused as she took a moment to contemplate, "These are the most difficult things to do, and not everyone can do it, not the weak."

"The soldiers should leave, they have brought nothing with them but hatred, and how can they protect us, when they see us as inferior, when they come with no compassion," said Nadda.

And with this both women worked for a while in the silence, both concentrating, trying to forget their surroundings. They were trying to forget what they heard, what they saw and what they lived. Nadda soon bid Sarah farewell and went home. A long day of hard work had passed, Sarah worked till sunset and till she couldn't stand any longer. She looked outside through the window, mesmerized by the full moon that had intruded upon the orange skies.

After she had finished her prayers, she sat down on her mat in silence, but, the quietness of it all had perturbed her. Normally the TV would be on at this time. The electricity was working again and it was time for Ali's favourite cartoon.

"Ali? Where are you?" She heard nothing, her ears drowned by the beating of her heart. "Ali!" she shouted, now panting. There was no reply; her palms began to sweat. She quickly stood up, jolting to her feet and sprinting through her house looking for her son. She continued to shout her son's name, but nothing responded. She heard nothing and with each shout her heart grew emptier, and her mind fell deeper, thinking of the possibilities. She looked everywhere, all around the house and yet found nothing. The toys were thrown to the ground and when she came to the kitchen, she found the door open, and she felt a sharp blade slice at her heart. What could have happened to her son? And why had he gone outside at this time?

Sarah searched the garden, she found no one. On the ground there was a fresh pool of blood, glimmering in the auburn sky; as red as the sun and as chilling as the moon. She gasped and held her breath. She tried to deny what she saw as tears streamed down her face. She called Nadda and asked her if she had seen little Ali, but she hadn't.

After a few minutes had passed, she had the whole street looking for him, and yet no one found him. She could hear the men whispering amongst each other, saying that he must have been kidnapped. Finally they found a witness, it was another child who had been looking outside his window. He told them that he had seen a man carrying an unconscious child. Tears gushed down Sarah's face, everyone on her street began driving around the neighbourhood looking for Ali. She couldn't afford a car, so she went inside Nadda's car. She screamed to the sky asking for the intervention of God. No prayer she said comforted her, no matter how many tears were shed, nothing happened.

After several hours of driving through the streets, she went back home hoping to see him returned. But nothing welcomed her back, except for that dreaded pool of blood, which was now covered by insects. Weeping and crying she reached for the blood, her hand covered in it, she began to smother her face with the blood of the child that lit her world, the child that gave meaning to her life. Even though she had the body of an old woman, at that moment, she saw herself for what she truly was; she still was a little girl. And yet her neighbours could do nothing. It was too much for her to handle, she couldn't stop thinking about her son and remembering how she cared and nurtured him. She cried till she dropped unconscious.

Chapter 2

Toska

Soft tapping against the window shakes Sarah as she passes in and out of sleep. She lies tossing and turning on her bed; a new day had begun. Her eyes shuddering from the bright lights, caught in the throngs of strange dreams, she forces one of her eyes open to see what the tapping is. The tapping continues and as she looks around, she could see a small insect endlessly flying against the window, flying and crashing against the window, hypnotized by the light of the dawn. Sarah heard a whispering in her head, and then a deep and menacing laughter.

"Do you seek the light?" the voice whispered ominously.

"Who is that?" asked Sarah into the darkness as the echoes of laughter surrounded her.

Before Sarah's eyelids materialized what appeared to be moving blobs, multi coloured apparitions, taking the shape of her house, the people she knew, different plants and insects. The apparitions danced in the darkness, morphing and changing.

"Who goes there?" she shouted once more, and whilst she did this the apparitions suddenly shook and took the shape of a cave. This cave glistened in the blue moonlight of this new world. It seems so real, she wondered to herself. She stood before the cave in trepidation, looking into it, and trying to make out what lay within. It was too dark, she could make nothing of it, and the longer she peered into this darkness the more it felt as if the darkness peered back at her. A voice thundered from within.

"Welcome, please come in," said the voice.

She gasped in shock, her knees shaking and her palms sweating profusely.

"But I can't see anything, it is too dark, I will get lost," she shouted back into the cave.

"When weren't you lost? When were you able to see anything?" the voice echoed. Sarah took a huge breath and began by slowly dipping her toes into this strange darkness. She could tell that this wasn't any normal cave. She took a slow step taking her foot and pressing it against the cave's surface; the ground here felt very smooth, almost like silk. She walked a few small steps and once more shouted, "I cannot see anything."

And once more the voice responded, "When were you ever able to see anything?" so she proceeded to walk into this darkness, trying to let go of her fears.

When she felt she had reached the centre of this cave she stopped. No light shone here, its silence as shattering as its mystery.

"Reveal yourself," she said.

"As you wish," the voice responded. For a moment, nothing happened. She began to doubt anything was going to happen, when suddenly, red crimson eyes grew from within this abyss, slowly and surely they increased in size. They were blood red, shaking with fervour, and dancing like the flame of a candle. Sarah was shaken by this; their intensity was strong sending her back a few steps and forcing her to recoil like a small child. They felt strangely familiar, yet at the same time there was a strong urge to look away.

"You cannot ignore me," spoke the red eyes.

"Who and what are you?" she asked.

"I am the truth and the lies. I am the swaying pendulum of the arbitrary reality that you cherish. I am what you truly are. I am you, just as you are me," spoke the mysterious eyes.

"Where have you come from?" asked Sarah.

"I have come from a place that no living being has ever seen. I come from the catacombs of immortality, and most importantly, I have come from the source. I have come from the numinous inspiration of my master; I have come from within you."

"Reveal yourself completely," spoke Sarah.

"But I fear that my form will scare you."

"I have lost all that is important to me, I cannot afford to be afraid anymore, reveal yourself," she requested once again.

"I am not allowed by decree to do such a thing. Only you may uncover me," explained the strange figure.

"And how do I do this?"

"Illuminate the darkness with your will, only those with pure hearts can meet me. Only those with the highest of aspirations are worthy of seeing me."

Sarah began to pray and just as soon as she had begun, her prayers were answered. A small lamp had materialized from thin air. Constructed from pure gold she was enthralled by its beauty.

She reached for it lifting it up, yet strangely it weighed very little and was easy to lift. Within it burned a small white flame that illuminated the darkness around where Sarah stood. The flame was dim so it was not powerful enough for her to see everything around her, yet it was enough for her to make out the dark figure that stood before her. She squinted trying to concentrate; her pupils constricting as she laid gaze upon the figure. Before her she saw a large Serpent. It was a large black Serpent, its skull larger than Sarah's body. Sarah dropped the lantern in shock and took a step back; once more all she could see were the crimson eyes looking back at her.

"Will you give up?" asked the Serpent.

Sarah knelt and lifted the lamp once more, and again illuminated the area around her. This time she did not avert her gaze. This time she took to investigating this giant creature, its skin like soot, its eyes piercing like a sharp blade. Its twin tipped tongue flickered against her body; she gave it no notice as she walked around it. The Serpent hung from a massive egg that it had coiled around.

"What are you holding onto?" asked Sarah.

"Shouldn't you ask yourself that question?" spoke the Serpent.

"Just tell me what is that huge egg for?" again asked Sarah.

"It contains what you're looking for, it encloses your understanding. That is all I will tell you, you will learn more when you're ready," spoke the Serpent.

"I want to learn and grow. I want to understand the world and who I am."

"Then you must learn to conquer your fears," said the Serpent, and then it proceeded to open its mouth. Its jaw large and wide, Sarah stared deep into it. A strange mist emanated out from the Serpent's mouth and filled the atmosphere, ascending like incense smoke. The string like mist rose to the sky whilst the Serpent whispered, "Enter".

Something strange came over Sarah. It was a strange nostalgia, looking deep within the Serpent's mouth. She took her first step, she knew it was insane, she knew it was dangerous, but she felt like she needed to. Ignoring the misty smoke and the flickering of the snake's tongue, she entered into the Serpent's mouth.

It's like a cave within a cave, a darkness within a darkness, Sarah thought to herself. Once she had walked deep enough, the Serpent's voice echoed around her, "Illuminate the darkness!"

And as she had done before she willed the lamp to lighten the place, there she stood looking deep into the darkness, trying to discern what stood before her.

Ali's voice rang through her, "Mummy" she could hear him as clear as crystal. She looked around and could find nothing.

"Over here," she heard his voice again, this time ringing from behind her, she stuttered then swiftly turned to look and again found nothing.

"Walk deeper!" she heard Ali say. With this she began to run deeper and deeper into the dark snake.

"You must stop! Do not go further. I cannot contain this much activity!" the Serpent's voice thundered. She gave it no notice and continued to dash into the depths. There she saw her son sitting down smiling at her. Her face ran with tears and her heart stopped, she took a deep breath and sighed. She rushed towards him, holding her arms out, when suddenly she felt a strong force tug on her right foot. Her body crashed against the silky entrance of the Serpent's jaw as he threw her out with his tongue and closed his mouth.

"Give him back to me!" exclaimed Sarah.

"I was not the one who took him," said the Serpent.

"Who took him? I want my son!"

"I cannot tell you that, but what I can do is help you."

The crowing of a rooster woke Sarah up, shocking her awake. She just sat up on her bed shaking, sweating profusely, staring at the wall and shielding her eyes from the sunlight. For a few seconds Sarah did not know where she was. She was still hurt by what had happened the day before, a lingering pain still remained in her heart, but the strange visions that she saw confused her.

"Ali! Are you there?" she could no longer tell reality from dream. Once again she realized what had happened; she burst into tears. Nadda heard her cries and rushed in to comfort her. She hugged Sarah and tried to quiet her down, but to no avail.

"Why am I back here, why have I returned to this existence, I have nothing to live for," sobbed Sarah. Nadda did not know what to say, all she could do was hug her friend. A day had passed, Sarah did nothing that day, and she spent the whole day glaring at the wall. She walked around her house finding Ali's old toys and crying. She couldn't step outside scared to see that puddle of blood. Nadda had cleaned it, but Sarah didn't know that; her house had become a prison.

It was night time now and Sarah was tired, her tear ducts were dry. Nadda knocked on the door, "It is open," said Sarah. Nadda walked in.

"We have spoken to your uncle in Najjaf and he was very upset and disturbed about what happened. He said he wanted you to come and live with him, it's much safer there," said Nadda. Sarah took a moment to think.

Chapter 3

The Voice

Sarah put more bread into the oven and embraced the whiplash of the flames. She had spent three days crying and lying around doing nothing, however now she spent her time baking bread. Her job had become second nature, automatic; an unconscious process. It was a kind of sleep waking. She blamed herself for what happened to Ali.

A few week had passed since her son was lost and since she declined her uncle Raheem's offer; she didn't really have a goal in mind. Her uncle had been living with her; he spent money and resources sending out people to look for Ali. Today however, he had to leave Sarah and return home. The streets were covered in a chilling silence, and by two o'clock everyone was home, by six they could hear gunfire.

The car had pulled up before Sarah's house; her uncle had his luggage at the entrance ready. They embraced at the door, "I will do whatever I can to help you, if you ever feel lost, if you ever feel sad, call me and I will come to you. Remember you have people who love and care about you, we will try our best to find Ali."

"Thank you," said Sarah as she stared coldly at the ground, her eyes as empty as her limbs that flailed to her sides. Her uncle noticed this and took a deep sigh.

"You know, everything happens for a reason," said her uncle as he embraced her.

"How do you mean?"

"Everything happens by the will of God. And know that even though you feel pain now, even though you feel that the world is dark and ugly, a day will come, and in that day your voice will echo through the hearts of men, and your actions will be immortalised by the love of God."

"But my son…"

"I know, just hold on, things will one day get better. We will find him, we will do everything that we are capable of," said Raheem as he kissed her forehead. He picked up his luggage and left. When his car had departed, Nadda could be seen in the distance throwing water behind the accelerating car. Doing this was thought to help form a kind of protection, from evil and from death. As the car drove off, a small rainbow formed behind it. The light of the sunset dispersed through the small spherical blobs of water that hung in the air. Sarah looked at this contemplating her uncle's words.

"To live a true life," she whispered to herself, "Our lives are defined by our actions. Whether the world is sheathed in darkness or covered in flames, we live…"

The world became insignificant, almost like an illusion, materialism felt petty and small. "The soul will never die…" again Sarah whispered to herself.

Sarah returned to her furnace to bake the bread, she was still in a state of shock, as an epiphany of sorts took over. Wrapped in profound thoughts she could no longer feel the heat of the flame, the rebound of the fire from the furnace no longer bothered her. Hypnotized by the fire, she was consumed by the serpentine flickering of the flame. Now she understood that the pain of the physical is nothing compared to the pain of regret, compared to the feelings of emptiness and depression.

"If I could only do something, if only I was to try, just try, wouldn't I have lived a meaningful life?" she spoke to the fire as if it were sentient. The fire felt alive, she did not feel lonely anymore; the world was alive. From the trees, the birds, the skies and every single atom around her.

As Sarah worked, neighbours came to purchase more bread and offer their condolences, they offered her money and charity, but she took none of it, and at the rates she was charging she was not making a profit. She done her job because she loved it, she would reminisce about the days she spent as a child, watching her mother bake pastries, smelling the sweet scent of newly baked bread.

"Why didn't you go with your uncle in Najjaf," said Nadda from the doorway as she entered.

"It wouldn't do me any good, I lived here my whole life, I can't go there, I won't let them scare me off. I have nothing to lose."

"Well, when you finish work I want you to come over for lunch, join me and my family. You can not spend the whole day on your own." As Nadda walked away and Sarah worked, Sarah began to think. She wasn't young anymore, she was old. Time was passing by, and she didn't feel it. Thinking back, the past felt so close. All those years had gone and she realized that through all those years, she had been sleep walking through life. She looked at the dough as it slowly transformed into bread, slowly growing, browning and becoming crisp.

"A transformation, yes, to change, to change my life..." said Sarah to the flames. It astonished her that her past, the days that she spent playing as a child up until this point, felt like a few days. From flying kite's, to marrying her husband, to her son's birth, all felt as if yesterday. The fire in the furnace kept burning, flickering and jolting about like a phoenix.

Just a few days ago Sarah had held a blade against her throat and contemplated suicide; a few days ago she thought that there was nothing left to do but die, but now she was thinking.

"Ali could still be out there, there are children out there dying, people out there helpless."

These thoughts, these ideas, they gave her reason to live; now she had shed her skin, and rose from the ashes. Quickly she finished work, closing everything. Locking the doors and rushing to Nadda's house. She sat with Nadda and her family. Sarah ate with haste, shovelling food into her mouth. Life was too short to waste, too short to spend sulking.

"Relax, slow down," said Nadda shocked by Sarah's voracity.

"I realized," said Sarah as she gulped her food without chewing it, "I finally realised the truth about life, how I should live my life," she said unintelligibly.

After they had finished their meal, Sarah took Nadda outside to the small garden behind her house. They played there as kids, and whenever Sarah or Nadda had something to say, they would always come here, look at the sky and talk. There were two large rocks in this garden; they used to sit on them as children and talk, so they never bothered to remove them. As they sat, Nadda noticed Sarah's caprice as she fidgeted and stared up at the stars. Nadda looked at Sarah thinking to herself, that maybe what had happened to her was too much to handle, maybe Sarah was not thinking normally.

"You look scared," said Sarah taking notice of Nadda's expression.

"How am I scared?"

"I know you too well, that look in your eyes, that squinting, how you scrunch your face." Nadda tried smiling, trying to relax the tense muscles in her face.

"Please don't be scared..."

"What's wrong?" asked Nadda.

"I have decided to leave this place," said Sarah.

"You're going to live in Najjaf?"

"No, I will go and look for my son. I can feel it, he's alive, I don't know how or why, but I can hear his heartbeat, I can hear his voice silently whispering my name. I can see what I must do, I've got to do this, and I'm going to get him back," Nadda sat there in shock biting her finger nails.

"It's too dangerous, you can't, you're not thinking straight." A moment passed as a cold breeze blew their hair, the sound of the hissing insects eclipsed by the sound of gunfire.

"I can't stay here any longer, I just can't, I can't live my life helpless, it is time for me to stand up."

"You've heard what the terrorists do to women they find on their own? Think carefully," cautioned Nadda.

"I will change the world, I will change my world and their world, and I want to see what I can do."

"But we are just women, what can we do?" explained Nadda. Sarah stood up staring at the beautiful night's sky, the stars glistening, the full moon shining brightly.

"Can our voices be heard? Does the government care? Do the people of the world care? Our people wait for divine intervention, but what are they waiting for? Aren't we as divine as any other thing of this world? I want them to see my actions, though my words did nothing to sway their ignorance, my actions will shatter it." Sarah's words were powerful, Nadda had never heard so much conviction in her friend's voice before, she looked up, joining her friend as they gazed at the sky.

"I don't think anything I say or do will change your mind," said Nadda as she led Sarah back inside. Nadda stopped at the door looking Sarah in the eyes, "And when you find your son, and you find the man who took him, what then?"

"I don't know, I just don't know."

"When do you plan to leave?" asked Nadda.

"As soon as I can," both of the women went their way, Nadda to look after her family, and Sarah to prepare for her journey.

It was eleven o'clock when Sarah went to bed. She had prepared a small bag for her travels, taking all of her life's savings with her. She lay on the mattress, she lay there thinking about her trip, imagining herself hugging her son. A tear of joy rolled down her face as she fell into a deep sleep.

She felt like she was descending into an abyss, the same nostalgia filled darkness that she had seen weeks ago. Once again blobs and apparitions began to appear before her, shifting their shape and constantly changing hue. Before she knew it, she was once again descending into a dark cave, floating down to the ground like a leaf, her toe gently touching the surface as she fell. She looked down at her feet, finding the lamp that she had left a week before. Sarah picked up the lamp and as she did, the lamp once again began to shine a light.

Before her stood the Serpent, as he was, still coiled around the egg. His nefarious eyes shone blood red through the darkness. Sarah stood there melancholically looking at the Serpent, and once again inspecting him.

"Déjà vu," whispered the Serpent as he lowered his head in line with Sarah's body. "You seem different," he continued, "I can not tell what, but you feel different."

"Where is my son?"

"Relax, you will find him soon, in fact you have already found him," said the Serpent smirking.

"What do you mean?"

"Time is not linear," he replied. Sarah stood there confused, "Don't worry, if you walk the correct path and follow your heart, you will eventually see your son."

"What is your name?" asked Sarah.

"My name is Azkazeal," said the Serpent with pride.

"And what do you do?" asked Sarah.

"I am the great conduit. I bring the infinite into the hands of the finite, and place the finite into the hands of the infinite." Sarah said nothing as she took a moment to think. "Sarah, you are here for a reason, you are here because you chose to come here, follow my advice and heed my warnings, with me by your side all doors shall open. But if you ignore me and my warnings," said Azkazeal as he revealed his fangs, "You will fall, and I won't be able to help you. The venomous nature of your own mind will devour you."

"I understand, but what do you want me to do now?"

"We need to agree on a contract, an oath, so that we may both be set free."

"What does the agreement entail?" asked Sarah.

"It entails finding your son, it entails my freedom," Azkazeal said this as his body slowly slithered stretching away from the egg; now only the lower part of his body was coiled around the egg. He formed a circle around Sarah and perched his head looking at her. Azkazeal then proceeded to close his eyes, and his forehead began to glow with strange silvery symbols. The floor on which Sarah stood began to glow with luminous light. Sarah looked around, amazed by the Serpent's strange powers.

"What are you doing? How are you doing this?"

"There is no time to waste Sarah; this agreement can only be carried out during a specific time."

"What's so special about this time?"

"You're mind needs to be at the zenith of concentration, and when this occurs; unus mundus," Sarah smiled at this, amused by the psychological jargon.

"How long will this take?" Sarah said as she sat on the floor crossed legged, placing the lamp by her side.

"Just be patient, we have to wait for the right time; when you are ready."

"How will I know when I'm ready?"

"You will feel a strange calm."

And for a while both Sarah and the Serpent sat in a silence, neither speaking. Both waiting, just waiting. Waiting for a moment, a moment they have yet to be familiar with.

"For now we should agree on the terms whilst we have the time."

"I want guidance," said Sarah, "I want to see my son."

"And I want purification," replied Azkazeal.

At that moment, Azkazeal's forehead began to emit a strong light, and the symbols on his skin enflamed with a blue neon tinge; the ground that they stood on began to shake. With his eyes closed, Azkazeal began to speak in tongues, his twin tipped tongue whipping around as he spoke a language Sarah did not understand. A hissing sound could be heard from the ground, and the skies within this dark world thundered. Smoke began to ascend, and a thick mist surrounded them, weakening their vision and creating hazy silhouettes. The smoke smelt strange, something otherworldly.

A sudden wind began to blow, sending Sarah's hair fluttering and getting in her eyes. The lamp began to roll away as this small hurricane sent the smoke spiralling out of control. Sarah reached for the lamp but couldn't get to it; she stood up falling several times, trying to push herself against this strong wind. Walking to the lamp she picked it up and brought it back down. She looked at the lamp; it was burning as bright as ever.

"Azkazeal, what do I do?" Sarah tried shouting through the mass chaos that surrounded her. However Azkazeal gave no notice, and continued talking in that strange language. His eyes closed, his skin glowing with strange and mystical symbols. Again Sarah shouted to Azkazeal trying to understand what was happening.

"This is the storm before the calm. Stay strong, close your eyes and relax," taking his advice Sarah closed her eyes as she ignored the chaos. Now she was trapped in a three-fold darkness, not only was she sitting in the darkness of this strange cave, and in a deep slumber, but she was also in the darkest parts of her own mind. A voice then began to thunder about the cave, speaking in unison with Azkazeal, in this strange language.

"Name your intentions, what is your path?" spoke this voice.

"I desire purification through her actions; I desire ascension," responded Azkazeal.

"And the cage of flesh?" asked the voice.

"I want to find my son, I want to understand the purpose of my existence," requested Sarah.

"Crystalized it shall be, to walk the path of destiny. You walk between the abyss and light, trapped in an eternal fight, however now you are blessed with sight, and with love shall you unite," said the voice.

An explosion of mist and air thundered through this world. Smoke and debris flew away as Sarah shielded her ears. The wind settled, and the glowing symbols of light upon Azkazeal's skin grew dim.

"Is it over?" asked Sarah. She heard no response, she looked back and saw Azkazeal's head lying on the ground with closed eyes, and his tongue lying to the side.

"Azkazeal, what should I do?" the Serpent gave no response.

"Azkazeal?" Sarah stood up walking towards the unconscious Serpent. She grabbed his tongue and tugged at it. His head jolted upwards as he gasped awake.

"There is no time to explain Sarah, you must leave now. You must go to the outer world and go south."

"South? Why would I go south?"

"It cannot be explained, you must listen to me," spoke the Serpent.

"But I want answers. I need to know what just happened; I need to know where I am going and why."

"The world does not work like that; it's not based on human logic. You must travel south to fulfil your destiny."

"How do I find my destiny there?"

"You don't need to look for it, as long as you pursue it, it shall also pursue you," said Azkazeal. "Quickly you must go now, I can sense danger and it is." But before the Serpent had time to finish what he was saying, Sarah found herself springing up and sitting on her bed, sweat ran down her face yet her body was cold. Her elbows dug into the mattress and her hands supported her head. She closed her eyes and took a deep sigh of relief. She could still see the after image of the Serpent clutching the mysterious egg. And just as soon as the afterimage had disappeared, she had forgotten about her encounter with the Serpent. She knew that there was something she'd forgotten, she knew it was important, but no matter how much she tried, she couldn't remember anymore.

She questioned this strange and unexplainable drive, that voice in the back of her head that told her to go south, yet she could not understand why or where it came from. "Significance…" a dull voice kept whispering in her mind. She got up and began packing her bag, preparing for a sporadic journey, an unplanned journey, one to take her into the centre of the world, and most importantly, to her son.

She didn't know where she was going, but she knew what she wanted to do. She was going to search for him. She was going to help the orphans and the needy. She wanted the politicians to see her, to understand her, and fear her. She thought to herself, that even if she left a small mark on the world, it would at least be her mark. She saw the world differently now, nothing was insignificant, from the smallest particle, to a grain of rice, to an ant, all were equally significant; all were filled with purpose.

She felt relieved; she did not want to rely on other people any longer. It was her duty as a mother, to go and find her son. When she had packed her bag, she tiptoed out of the house and like a phantom, she made no noise. She left the house and walked away from her shelter; she walked away from comfort and entered the sandy concrete chaos of Baghdad. She left, looking for the wolves.

Sarah walked past torn buildings. She walked past old infrastructures, now brought to the ground. What used to be great steel constructions, edifices that had once lifted the aspirations of men, were now crushed. The shattered glass crackling beneath her feet and glimmered in the starlight, she walked through Baghdad, hearing faint screams and gunfire ring through the city. She looked up seeing a flurry of bats flying through the night's sky. The scorpions and snakes crawled through the harsh desert sand, and what was once a radiant advent for culture and intellect, was now but a hell that none could escape, she however continued.

Her eyes were as dry as the sand she now walked upon. To the south she walked, the cold air freezing and electrifying her skin, she pushed against it as the shards of pain spread through her body. "Tears and crying, that's what Iraq has become," she thought to herself, "But I have hope, I have a will, I have a voice."

Chapter 4

The Journey

As Sarah walked the starry night, she contemplated God and his existence. Her faith had been bruised, and she questioned what it meant to be alive. Perhaps I've already died and this is my hell, my punishment, she thought to herself. She came to the realization that death was inevitable, that there must be a law out there, some divine law, something she could rely on. Her limbs were now weak; she had been walking for hours. The wind was bellowing forcing her *abaya* to flutter and block her eyes.

The *abaya* was camouflaging her within the darkness. Cars would pass her, militias and tanks would roll by, but she was invisible. The darkness had become her safety, her haven. The militias and gangs would drive by her, clutching their weapons. They would scream, and she could hear their foul language fill the silence. She could see them clearly, yet they could not see her.

This was the first time Sarah had felt so much power. She had a goal. She had always relied on others, but for the first time someone relied on her, her son, her soul and Azkazeal. "I am sorry oh dear son," she would whisper under her breath, as every now and then a fleeting moment of regret would overcome her.

Azkazeal's advice was strange; she felt that there was hidden wisdom in his guidance. She was guided by an unseen force, a divine presence that permeated all matter and beings. Her path revealed to her many things. She walked past many houses and many different people, her heart beating nervously, knowing that if someone saw her, a lone women walking through Baghdad in the night; that she would be killed or worse.

Looking around her in contemplation, everything just fit and made sense, from the rising of the sun over the horizon, to the ant carrying a leaf back to its base. Walking in that direction became second nature.

After several more hours, she had reached the true desert; there were no lights, no humans, just the pure and cold shattering starry night. Sarah felt as if she was walking through snow. She saw the sun perform its daily revelation, appearing from the dark horizon, its orange tinge bringing the desert to life. Sarah stopped, and opened her small bag to eat some bread and drink water. She began to pray, asking for protection and for guidance. She performed her ablution with the cold desert sand instead of water, but to her, she could not tell the difference, the cold night had practically frozen the earth.

Up ahead, she could see a small village. Covered by sandstorms it looked as if it were a lost civilization. Sarah eventually fell to the ground, hoping to catch her breath; she stared at the distant town in awe. She looked at it wondering and trying to understand her journey. It was like a movie, she thought to herself. It seemed almost unreal; she was traversing difficult terrain, a lone woman looking for her kidnapped son. The more she thought about it, the more depressed she got, because she did not know what to do. She did not know how she was to find Ali, and in her current state she had forgotten why she was walking south anyway.

The thoughts and emotions faded as fast as they had manifested, and once more Sarah found herself soothed by the whistling of the wind. And so she fell asleep in the middle of the desert, the snakes and scorpions gave her no attention, they scurried and slithered by her as she lay in a deep slumber.

The rooster's crowing shook Sarah awake and she once again stood up to walk her path. Sarah approached the small village walking amongst the broken houses and the tank crushed cars. The stench of rotting corpses and flowing blood tingled in Sarah's nostrils. It was an impoverished village, being used as a haven for nefarious purposes. When she could smell the scent of death and when she saw the packs of malnourished children kneeling in the gutters, she knew for that moment that what lead her to this destination was not random, it was fate.

"Hey, where are you going?" a voice sounded from above her.

"Who are you? How can I hear you?" Sarah spoke to the skies.

"I'm just a regular guy," replied the voice.

"How can you see me?" she asked trying to understand this numinous figure.

"Over here," laughed the voice. Sarah looked around, searching the area from which the voice sounded.

"Here, look at me," said the voice; Sarah began searching the area only to see an old man hanging from a date palm tree. He looked like he was in his eighties, with toned muscles and wrinkly skin. He had his head wrapped with a *keffiyeh*, he was high up on the tree. He had created a sling, wrapping it around the tree and staying high up by pushing himself with his feet as it cradled his arched back.

"I am not God, or at least I don't think I am," laughed the old man.

"You scared me."

"What brings you to this town, this place is dangerous," warned the old man.

"The same thing that brought you here."

"And what's that?"

"God brought me here," she said.

"God? God brought you here?" said the old man laughing, "Most people that come here were brought here by the devil."

"I'd like to meet these people," said Sarah.

"I see…" the old man scratched his head and readjusted his *keffiyeh*, "You came here searching for the devil?"

"You could say that…" said Sarah.

"I'm saying this to protect you, leave, leave while you still can."

"If I could leave this place, I would, but it took something from me, this place doesn't want to leave me, so I won't leave either," said Sarah. "I want to stay for a while."

"This village is poor, there are very few places that get any electricity, and also the water here is scarce and dirty. Many people that used to live here have either fled or have been murdered in meaningless clashes. Some still protest against the government, others stay hidden in their concrete tombs. There are various foreign thugs operating here. And many countries send their secret services to this location; this place is used as a rendezvous point for many different people."

Sarah took a moment to process all of this information, "Why do you tell me all of this?" she asked.

"I don't know why I'm telling you, I just feel like I have to," said the old man.

"What else should I know?" asked Sarah.

"Many of the young men here have also become criminals and thugs. According to them, why should they spend their time begging the governmental thieves, when they could just take it by force? I've tried talking to them, there's just no way you can succeed. To some degree they are right, the government itself is corrupt, so what are they to do… Just be careful, that is all I'm trying to say."

"Thank you for the warnings," said Sarah. The old man bid her farewell as she made her way deeper into the town. As Sarah walked through this town the children eyed her, but refrained from begging her for any food. She didn't look particularly rich, her ravished and simplistic clothes and her tattered and sandy *abaya* made her fit in.

Kidnappings had become a lucrative business venture, albeit a dangerous one. Foreign masters, hidden leaders, veiled behind the guise of righteousness were in reality malevolent. Those that toted the flag of religion done so for their own greedy benefits in mind. Each decapitated head brought before the *Amir* or "Master" of these criminal organizations, earned the murderer a large sum of money. Sarah thought about these things as she perused the area. She knew that those who claimed to fight for religion were her enemy. Their ignorance had murdered their humanity, why else would they travel miles into another man's land and blow themselves up?

She had made a promise to Azkazeal, that she would purify him. She knew that by changing herself, she could change the world. For how can anyone create light, when they themselves are living in the darkness, when their very own internal demons could destroy them from within?

Snapping out of her daydream, Sarah's gaze locked onto a small orphan girl's eyes, she was sitting down on the ground curled up into a little ball, shielding her eyes behind her forearms and knees. Sarah began to unpack her bag, all the children ran around her, looking and jumping about. The older children pushed and shoved, tugging on Sarah's *abaya*.

"Come on now, relax," she said. "Everyone will get some."

But they did not listen, they were climbing on top of her, Sarah was laughing as their small hands and feet dug into her and rushed around her body, tickling her. The loud commotion had soon descended into a silence; the children took their time to enjoy the food. Sarah looked at them smiling, within each of them she saw aspects of her son. At least her son had someone that showed him love, she thought, she has people looking for him. Seeing the beauty and harmony that she brought into the world comforted her. Most of the children were now well fed, and Sarah had now run out of food to give. She closed her bag and continued her search in this strange and forsaken village. However, as she walked away, a pattering noise could be heard following her like a shadow.

It was the pattering of small feet. She looked behind her and found that small girl that she had approached now following her. The little girl held in her hand a small soft toy. She held it and followed Sarah smiling. Sarah kept an eye on this little girl as she walked across the village.

The small child continued to follow Sarah; however Sarah did not want a companion on her journey, for she knew that her quest would be a dangerous one. Maybe it would be safer if she came with me, Sarah pondered. She turned around and confronted the child; kneeling and talking with the girl eye to eye.

"My name is Sarah, what's your name?"

The girl did not respond, she stared back blankly at Sarah.

"Do you have a name?" asked Sarah once more.

The girl stretched out her arm; Sarah took her little hand and found a small ring that the little girl was wearing.

"What's this?" said Sarah as she tried to pull the ring off the girl's finger. But the small girl squirmed and cried, she pulled her arm away.

"It's Okay," said Sarah in a hushed voice, "I won't take it off." She handled the girl's tiny hands delicately, and inspected the ring. Upon the ring Sarah found an engraving, the name: Nahrayn.

"Your name is Nahrayn?" asked Sarah.

Nahrayn smiled.

"Where's your mummy and daddy?"

Nahrayn began to shake her head, shrugging.

"You don't know where your parents are?" asked Sarah.

Nahrayn looked back silently.

"Don't you have any family?"

Nahrayn looked down to the ground.

Sarah picked up the small child; she put Nahrayn on her lap and spoke to her softly.

"You can't come with me, it is dangerous," said Sarah to Nahrayn.

Nahrayn hugged Sarah, closing her eyes, Nahrayn was lost in a new world; a world of affection. And Sarah could not reject the child. She could not leave her alone any longer. She was small and tiny, and she was younger than all the other kids.

"I suppose you can come with me, till I can find your home," said Sarah, Nahrayn smiled and jumped off Sarah's lap. Sarah picked her up as Nahrayn relaxed her head on Sarah's shoulder.

"How can you walk barefoot on these grounds? It's too hot." Nahrayn had never been lifted up before, she smiled and laughed. For once in her life she felt like she was on top of the world. She had been like a lone wolf, having to compete for food and water, and when she was ill, no one comforted her, all she did was await death's embrace. The suicidal thoughts that once lurked within Nahrayn's mind slowly faded, she never thought that things could get better. Beneath Sarah's glimmering smile she knew that she shouldn't have taken Nahrayn with her, she knew that her journey was dangerous and unpredictable. But when she looked into Nahrayn's eyes, she found hope, she found peace.

She could sense that her quest would not be a normal one. Still, the bliss and comfort she brought to Nahrayn sufficed for this, and for once in many days, Sarah's aching heart was soothed.

Sarah traversed the town asking questions. She walked the many roads of the town, and soon came upon a convoy of several trucks. Sarah looked at the gangs as they passed, she looked for her son, hoping that he may be in one of the trucks that passed by. Whenever the trucks did pass; Nahrayn would cringe, leaping off Sarah's shoulder and clinging onto Sarah's leg, hiding behind the fluttering *abaya*.

There was a small shop in this outrun district. Sarah took Nahrayn with her and entered the shop. The shop was very eclectic to say the least; it was filled with electrical products that looked like they were either stolen or smuggled into the country. The products located in this shop were varied, some old and some new. From food to clothing, all were stored and squeezed into every nook and crevice of the small shop. The shop-owner was a young man with expensive sunglasses and gelled hair. He must have either stolen or inherited the place, thought Sarah to herself; he was so young and so rich in a poor neighbourhood that it didn't make sense. She began scanning the shop and eventually found a small pair of sandals for Nahrayn.

"Just take them," said the young man before Sarah could ask their price. He was busy using his cell phone and fiddling with his beer cans.

"Thank you for the kindness," said Sarah. Nahrayn laughed and giggled as Sarah tickled her feet and slid the new sandals on her.

"Do you mind if I ask you some questions?" said Sarah to the young man.

"What do you want to tell me? I'm tired of all the religious talks," said the young man as he browsed through his phone. "I help people and live my life, I don't have to follow anyone else's way of life just to make them happy."

"No it's not about that, it's about this town," said Sarah.

"What do you want to know? This is a forgotten town. It is a wolves den. The government don't care, and the people are barely able to live."

"My son was kidnapped," said Sarah. The young man put his cell phone down and looked at Sarah with concern.

"I'm so sorry to hear that, do you think the people who kidnapped him brought him here?"

"I have a feeling that they did."

"What makes you say that?" asked the man curiously.

"It's a mother's intuition."

"Well I hope you're wrong, for your son's sake."

"Why do you say that?" she asked.

"To be in this town, you have to be well connected. You have to know everyone," said the young man. Sarah approached the young man as he sat on his desk.

"Who are these bad people?" she asked, but the young man didn't answer, he simply looked at her silently.

"Who are these people?" she asked once more.

"I don't know lady, all I know is that this is a regular kidnap location, just be very careful."

"I understand, you're scared of them, that is why you don't want to tell me?"

"You shouldn't go around chasing the wrong people, talk to the wrong people, and you die, this is how things are here. My advice to you is to take your daughter and pay someone to search for your son, or just pay the ransom."

"Ransom?" whispered Sarah, "I never received any phone calls or letters from the kidnappers, and I have no money."

"That's strange," replied the man as he scratched his head, "The notorious kidnappers known here all leave some kind of message for a ransom or a request."

Sarah thanked the man for the information and left the shop; she ignored his warnings and continued her search. Sarah walked through the town looking for food and water, the blaze of the sun crackling against her skull, and the air swaying in the heat. Through the blinding heat, she saw a woman walking hastily.

"Excuse me!" shouted Sarah to the woman, but the woman walked on ignoring her.

"Excuse me!" she shouted once more, hoping to capture the woman's attention. The woman looked back giving Sarah a small glance; Sarah could see the woman's eyes filled with fear.

"Water!" shouted Sarah, the woman stopped in her tracks, glimpsing back at Sarah and Nahrayn. The woman walked towards her; her face pale and her eyes empty and cold.

"Do you know where we can find water?" asked Sarah.

"You're not from her are you?" whispered the woman.

"No."

"What are you doing in this town? Do you know how dangerous it is here?"

"I am looking for my son."

"Another one of those?" whispered the woman to herself.

"Another one of what?"

"It's nothing," replied the woman, "Come with me, I know where you can find water." The woman began to walk, "Come on, it's dangerous to stand in the middle of the street."

She led Sarah behind a small house, there along the deserted garden, was a small tap of water protruding from the ground. The woman knelt next to the valve, twisting it.

"Water is hard to come by," she said as she continued to twist the valve frantically. Nahrayn skipped next to the woman, she knelt next to the tap inspecting it meticulously.

"Water is hard to come by?" asked Sarah.

"Yeah, ever since the neighbouring countries built big dams, very little water flows through her." answered the woman.

"So what do you do when you're thirsty?" asked Sarah.

"We wait."

They stood by the tap waiting. It then began to rumble and wheeze, and then water began to slowly drip out.

"So much for 'the land of the twin rivers'..." said the woman, "Drink quickly before it stops."

Sarah and Nahrayn drank from the tap; the water was warm and unappetizing. Yet that did little to stop them, and they did not notice it. After they had finished, Sarah took out a small plastic bottle and began to fill it up.

"Earlier, you said that there were others, what did you mean by that?" asked Sarah.

"It's nothing," said the woman.

Sarah stared back at the woman with an empty and cold face.

"It's just… I've seen a couple of parents show up here, they were looking for their children."

"Why do they come here? Is this place known for kidnappings?" asked Sarah.

"This place is known for a lot of things… When was you're son kidnapped?"

"A few weeks ago," she said teary eyed.

"I'm Amal," said the woman stretching forth her hand to Sarah.

"I'm Sarah," she greeted Amal.

Sarah felt Amal's hand shaking, noticing this Amal retracted her hand. The two women spoke to each other for that whole day; they talked about the town, the people, and their dreams. Amal was a woman living on her own in the town, she had a small house that her father had left her. Darkness soon fell upon the land, and the air had become cold.

"Come sleep in my house, I could use some guests," said Amal.

"If it's not too much hassle, I don't want to intrude."

"No please, I insist. I have a spare bed and you have nowhere to stay." Amal pressured her till she agreed to stay over at her house. When they got there, they nurtured Nahrayn, bathing her, feeding her and dressing her in clean clothes. Through all this, Nahrayn remained silent; and it was her silence that spoke of what her eyes had seen. Nonetheless she stayed quiet, watching the women talk amongst themselves. They sat on a woven wool carpet. When Nahrayn had fallen asleep, Sarah sat next to Amal, Amal brought small Arabic glasses of tea called an *estikaan*. She let the tea leaves slowly boil in the water and set them by Sarah.

"I sense a deep fear within you," said Sarah.

"A deep fear? What do you mean?"

"There is something, something you're scared of."

"We're all scared of something, and there are some people that you should be scared," responded Amal.

"Who should be scared?"

"You should, everyone should, because the world has changed."

"But why are you so afraid, why should I be afraid?" asked Sarah.

"A notorious murderer and kidnapper has been coming here regularly, whoever has seen him, doesn't live for very long," whispered Amal to

Sarah, "He is a madman who would stop at nothing to kill."

"What's his name?"

"We don't know... but people have begun calling him 'Tabbar', this is why I advise you to take heed," said Amal.

"We shouldn't be scared, fear will destroy us, I've been afraid for all of my life."

"Maybe this is why you're still alive..." said Amal.

"Is it living?" asked Sarah. "Am I really alive?"

Amal began filling the *estikaan* with tea, she knew it was just right, because the tea had a light brownish golden tinge to it and the leaves had descended to the bottom.

"This may be the most dangerous part of all Iraq. What brought you here?" asked Amal as she handed the tea to Sarah.

"Is it really dangerous? It's a small town, is it as bad as Baghdad?"

"It's very dangerous for that reason, it's small, it's a hideout, and secret dens lie hidden amongst the dunes and small homes. Dens of criminals and kidnappers, positions from where they conduct and manage their attacks. So Sarah, you have to tell me what brought you here?" Sarah looked back blankly. "You can tell me, who told you your son was here?" again Amal asked.

"I don't know… I can't remember."

"You have no idea why you came here?" Amal asked in awe.

"It is a mother's intuition, I can feel it. Tell me more about this 'Tabbar'."

"He's the new prince…" said Amal.

"Prince?" asked Sarah.

"Prince, it's a status used in these terrorist cults. After ten decapitations the decapitator is 'promoted', they have their own strange culture."

"Decapitation?" Sarah was in shock.

Amal noticed this and quieted down, she looked at Sarah and her reaction, "Don't worry, they don't decapitate children."

"What do they do with children?" Sarah Asked.

Amal looked to the ground, and took a sip of tea from her *estikaan*.

"Tell me."

"I don't know," replied Amal.

"You have to tell me!" insisted Sarah.

"It depends on who kidnapped whom. How much they are worth, and how much ransom can be obtained."

Sarah began to cry, tears slowly running down her cheeks. Amal held her, comforting her.

"You're son, he has a beautiful mother with a wonderful heart." Amal's words done little and Sarah continued to cry. "Please don't cry, don't give up. The universe won't let them live happy, money and power are their God, yours is love and justice. Never give up, never..."

"I won't," said Sarah as she wiped the tears from her eyes. The room was suddenly covered in darkness; the electricity had been cut.

"The generator isn't working anymore..." said Amal in a hushed voice. The two women couldn't see anything; Sarah could hear Amal sip tea from within the darkness.

"Is it going to take long?" asked Sarah.

"The electricity won't come back for some time. Did you always have electricity where you're from?"

"No, but my neighbour always let me use some from her generator."

Amal got up and opened up a nearby window, the tea shone in the moon light and the stars brightly sparkled from within the depths of the sky.

"Are you hungry?" asked Amal.

"A little bit."

"Here," said Amal walking back from the corner of the room with a tray of dates.

"You can't go hungry if you know where to look," said Amal smiling.

"They are very sweet."

"It's the same tree that I've been going to for years. I've been watering it since I was a little girl."

"That's good to hear," replied Sarah.

"Yeah I know; it's sad really, most of the trees and animals were destroyed by the wars."

After the women had finished eating and drinking their tea, Amal laid a mattress on the floor for Sarah.

"Thank you for all you've done."

"It's nothing."

As Sarah lay on her bed staring out the window, she contemplated, asking herself, why she was here, what had brought her here, what made her change? Was it because of her carelessness, was it someone else's fault. Why had her path crossed with Nahrayn's, why had she met Amal, she thought about these things, she thought of vengeance, fantasizing of finding the kidnappers, of shouting at them. The moon luminously glared from the window, silhouettes of bats in the sky formed by the moonlit Iraqi night's sky. To the bats the darkness was the light, and the light was the darkness.

She fell asleep picturing her son's face smiling back at her. She felt as if she was sinking into her bed, going deeper and deeper into sleep, into the darkness. It felt as if she were levitating, slowly descending into this darkness, smooth and soft wind sending her dress fluttering in the breeze as she stretched her toes down trying to find her feet. Soon she felt the tip of her toe press against the ground as dust swarmed and gathered around her in a minaret of mist.

Once again she stood in this dark platform, looking into the nothingness. Stretching her arms to the floor and trying to feel out a lamp, she finally finds something and lifts the lamp to her face. Grasping it with both hands, it was glowing and getting stronger, before her from within the darkness the dark Serpent was waiting. His tongue flickering about as he hung from the egg, the egg was glowing like silver, and yet Azkazeal done his best to encompass it so that none of its light may be seen. In this world there was nothing to see, nothing except her and this entity, which was almost difficult to make out; his skin was reflecting the flame of the lamp.

"Welcome oh light bearer," said Azkazeal, his looming head descending to her level. "Are you having trouble?" he asked.

"Trouble with what?"

"Trouble understanding the path that you walk. You now seek to change the world? Only when pain breaks the shell of your understanding, do you awaken."

"There are others still sleeping?" asked Sarah.

"Yes Sarah, humans love to be guided. But they never seek to follow their hearts. No, the masses follow the few, blindly. They do not understand that deep within themselves, lies all that they ever sought. Their true destiny is never fulfilled, and they spend their time seeking what others can offer them. But they do not understand, that other people will never offer them their destiny, and like a tree they are split asunder by the dogma of others. They are uprooted, they lose their way. And like a tree they are hacked and crafted into a ship, a collective that can cross oceans, one that can withstand the fury of the sea and of nature itself." said Azkazeal.

"Then like the tree, they were truly misled."

"And why is that?"

"When it was rooted within the earth, and when it had a mind of its own, it sought its own path; it moved towards the light," replied Sarah.

"You are right," spoke the Serpent impressed. "We all must walk our own path, none can be guided, The only true guidance, is the guidance provided by oneself. I see you have gained a considerable amount of knowledge. However tell me this Sarah, would you have gained this knowledge if you had not travelled, would have anything come about of your life if you did not suffer and bear the pain of your journey?"

Sarah looked back at him wearily, her voice shaking. "A part of me died that day, but also a new aspect was born. I don't know who I am anymore. Am I the young girl that played in the street when

I was young? The widow? Or a bereaved mother? I don't even know who those aspects of me were, I can't remember them, I can't..."

Azkazeal fell to a silence, his eyes closed and his head descending till it lay on the ground. Sarah looked on bamboozled at what was going on. Azkazeal's skin began to radiate, it began to shine. Slowly and surely, the egg that he coiled began to levitate, it ascended towards the sky. Sarah noticed the lamp beginning to glow ever brighter, she held it and looked at Azkazeal, he shone and stood there in the shadowy sky of this strange world. Behind Azkazeal the silvery egg was glowing, the light was so strong it could be seen through the Serpent's body.

The wind began to blow, forcing Sarah to clutch the ground and tighten her grip on the lamp, Azkazeal was floating high, and the wind was strong. Smoke and mist began to emanate from an unknown source making it difficult to see. A sweet scent permeated the air; however, Sarah was too busy trying to keep her footing to notice.

Azkazeal began to spin around the egg, like a motor; coiled and spinning, biting his tail and shining. Looking from afar Sarah stood in awe, seeing the revolving Serpent so high, at such speed, so bright, it was mesmerizing. The light grew till Sarah had to shield her eyes from its intensity. Eventually the wind quieted down, the light diminished, and when Sarah had uncovered her eyes, she saw Azkazeal descend. A fragment of his past lay on the dark floor; he had shed his skin. Sarah inspected the shed skin from afar, looking as dark as the shadows that enveloped it and eventually fading away not to be seen. Azkazeal's new skin was not as light consuming as the shed skin, this time it shone, it reflected, almost like a dark mirror. Deep within Azkazeal's eyes Sarah could see a look of content and peace, one that was not present before.

"You must continue your journey, you must always learn and grow," spoke Azkazeal as he tried to catch his breath.

"What happened?"

"My purification, the ascension."

"Was that it?" asked Sarah.

"No, that was but one of the many stages."

"Azkazeal, why is it so dark here?"

"It is dark because of him," spoke Azkazeal gesturing and pointing with his tongue behind Sarah. Sarah looked into the gloomy distance behind her and found nothing.

"I can't see anything," she said.

"Lift your lamp, and walk closer, concentrating there," so with that Sarah took to walking towards that direction bearing her lamp with her, and swaying it in front of her searching for something.

In the distance, high in the sky, something dark was there, something as dark as Azkazeal, yet silent. Sarah took a few steps back, a nostalgic fear shattered her; it left her petrified.

"Do not be scared, for fear will destroy you," said Azkazeal as he tried to reassure the woman. Taking each step slowly, she approached this mysterious silhouette, and what at first seemed like a random pattern in the sky, became discernible, there he was, another Serpent, floating in the dark sky. He also coiled around a spherical object. The mysterious Serpent, turned his head towards her, in his eyes was a look of complete melancholy. Sarah and this new Serpent looked at each other in the eye, and he slowly turned away, attempting to ignore her.

"Who is he?" asked Sarah.

"He is my brother, his name is Mazaroth," said Azkazeal.

"Why does he hang there, in the dark skies?"

"He dwells in the light, or what was once a light."

Sarah looked at Azkazeal in confusion.

"You asked why it is dark in this dimension. It is because of him; he encompasses the sun, and lets no thread of light pass so long as he lives."

"Why does he do this?"

"I do not know. I have tried talking with him, but it was futile, he simply hangs there locked in disdain and scorn for something he is not willing to talk about."

"But I want to experience the full wonders of this world," exclaimed Sarah like a little girl.

"If you seek to uncoil this mystery, then I suggest that you go and speak to him. Maybe you could understand what I could not."

Sarah took a deep breath and took her lamp in her hands, she looked at Mazaroth, and began to pace her steps, slowly approaching the strange new creature. Mazaroth looked as if in deep meditation, lost within the fury of the emptiness that he coveted.

"A caged one?" said Mazaroth as Sarah reached his abode.

"I hear from your brother that you are Mazaroth, the concealer of the light!" shouted Sarah looking up to Mazaroth in the sky.

"You have heard wrong, I am the protector of the weak and weary. I am the dark truth to all lights, and the big lie to all the darkness."

"And what do you do? Why are you here, why do you encompass that sphere?" asked Sarah. Mazaroth looked back, took a deep breath to compose himself, and his voice echoed all around her:

"I embrace the sun so bright
Just as the beating heart

Never sees the light
I can still hear the ringing
That echoes from the stars
A verse springing
A rendition of their scars
So I shield the truth
That causeth the pain
And keep you safe within this plane."

Sarah was confused, she had no time for riddles, or complex poetry and she knew her time was limited in this world.

"I'm sorry but I have very little time."

"You do not even understand time. Time is not something that could be had. Time is the souls travel through experiences. In essence your conception of space and time is limited," said Mazaroth.

"And how do you know all of this?"

"Because we are the timeless ones, we are what you will one day become," said Mazaroth.

"And why do you tell me all of this?"

"Because it was decreed that I speak these words, and it was decreed that you hear these words," he responded.

"Well then tell me, why do you shield the sun?" asked Sarah.

"Tis not I that shield the sun, what I am doing is simply protecting those who can't handle its effervescence. My master's ignorance, it weakens him, all humans were once made and intended to shine as the stars, but marred by their own ignorance, the light that they are bestowed with can blind them."

"Who is your master?"

"That I cannot say oh caged one," said Mazaroth.

"Why can't you say?"

"Because that is something that I wasn't decreed to say, and it was something you were not decreed to hear."

"Does the sun not burn your flesh? Does its vibrant light and power not harm you?" she asked.

"Only him who can completely enter and be engulfed in the darkness can bear this pain, I am the Promethean of my master, I am the titan that held the world, but one day, my master will not need my help any longer, I will be held up instead, I will be nourished by his new found wisdom."

Mazaroth's head descended in a slouch, and he began to whisper, "Until that time comes, the darkness has become the light, and the light has become the darkness." Sarah looked at him, her lips departed, her tongue touching the palate of her mouth, but before she could speak, Mazaroth interrupted, his body arching itself.

"The blood of your people is spilt daily. The land that you reside in was once our home, it still is our true home, but it is being ravished by ignorance and greed. The angels look down at you, but alas they can do nothing."

Sarah knew what Mazaroth spoke of; she knew that he alluded to her son, and the pain that any other innocent victim may experience in Mesopotamia.

"How do I find my son?" asked Sarah.

"The question isn't how you find him, but how you lost him."

"I lost him, it was not my intention to lose him, and it was an accident."

"In your world, there are no accidents, there are no coincidences, there are only experiences. Remember that the path you follow is your path. Even if you were to change it drastically, it would still be your path. Remember this as you search for your son. Remember who coils the one you think you see, and you will find the one that you seek."

Poetry and ambiguous speeches left much to be desired, but she knew what he was doing, Mazaroth liked to cover the truth in deceit, to dress the lies with flowery words. Like a bat that sought to fly in the day, she mingled with him, talking of reality and truth. This was his world; these were subject matters that he was more than familiar with.

"I will comeback one day, and the light that you guard will shine through you, it will reach this world," she said.

Sarah walked back to Azkazeal whilst waving goodbye to Mazaroth, she waved as if a young child would to an old relative. Azkazeal was smiling; he had a strange look about him.

"That was an intense conversation," said Azkazeal.

"What did you hear?" she asked.

"I heard everything."

"But how?" Sarah asked in astonishment.

"There are ways to listen and ways to understand, they go beyond your five senses oh Sarah. One of these senses you are more than familiar with, such as a mother's intuition."

"Whenever I come here, I leave with more things to think about. I leave with more questions than answers," said Sarah.

"That is a good thing. To understand something completely; and it loses its mystery, it loses its beauty. This is the grace of nature; its never ending secrets. You should try speaking with Mazaroth again soon. I sense that you have had a profound effect on him."

"Who is Mazaroth's master?"

"That I do not know. But what I do know, is that information gathered from him, is vital to your journey."

Chapter 5

A Lost Girl

Footsteps and the sound of hissing lulled Sarah out of her sleep; people could be heard gathering outside and whispering amongst each other. Being awoken so suddenly gave Sarah a splitting headache. The conversation she had been having with Azkazeal had disappeared. It was now considered by her as nothing but a mere dream, a figment of her imagination. The visions ceased as she listened carefully to the sounds around her.

Nahrayn was still asleep next to her when she got up. She snuck towards Amal's room trying to make as little sound as possible. When she had reached Amal, she lightly touched her on her shoulder, whispering: "Wake up". Sarah maintained her hushed voice, "Someone is outside, there are people outside."

Amal looked at Sarah in fear, she made no noise, she simply sat their in the dark, listening to the silence. She scurried to a nearby wall yet remained crouching. Amal opened a window, making sure to open it very slowly. She then started to gradually peek through the corner of the window. She wanted to see what was happening outside, but she was trying her best to avoid detection. The sound of gunfire echoed from afar and bullets began to graze the sides of the building. Sarah jumped towards Amal, flying through the air, grabbing her, and pulling her her down to the ground.

Amal wheezed for air as her chest slammed against the surface of the floor. They looked up at the window in fear. Several bullets smashed through the glass shattering it as well as the mental stability of the two women. Sarah reached up to the window; she stretched her hands and lightly pushed what was left of it so that it was closed.

The two women crawled away in fear; they crawled to the wall opposite. Sarah closed the door to where Nahrayn was asleep. After a few moments had passed, loud banging was heard coming from the front door. Sarah and Amal looked at each other with concern. Sarah began to crawl to the door but Amal grabbed hold of her arm.

"It is too dangerous," whispered Amal.

"We have no choice, whoever they are, they know we are here," Sarah whispered back. So they both crawled to the front door. Sarah got up slowly, unlocking the door. She placed her hands on the doorknob, but the door shook itself open, and a dark shadow stood before her. Sarah felt a large object smashing against her face; she fell to the ground writhing in pain. Amal could be heard screaming in the background. Sarah felt Amal's body atop hers, tugging and weeping.

"Stay down, don't get up!" was screamed into their ears in really bad Arabic. Wiping the blood from her face, she saw American soldiers standing at her door, in their hands large M16 rifles. The soldiers grabbed hold of the two women and pushed them against a wall.

"Don't move and stay quiet," a different voice spoke, this time in a native Iraqi dialect. A soldier rushed and began frisking the two women.

Amal cried, whilst Sarah was still recovering from the sudden fall. With their faces pressed against the wall they could hear soldiers going through the house and looking through shelves. Nahrayn could be heard crying awake in the other room. Nahrayn was rushed next to the women as she cried and wept, she hung onto Sarah's legs in fear.

The soldiers messed the rooms up; leaving a trail of mud and strewn clothes on the floor. Sofas were ripped open and the TV was thrown to the ground as they searched the small home.

"Stay calm," the native voice spoke once more, "The Americans are looking for a terrorist group from this area."

Sarah felt the tip of a rifle being pressed against her head, she moved her head away, but it was forced back into position.

"We aren't the terrorists!" cried Amal. "We are women, we are citizens."

"Be quiet," spoke the voice again in frustration. After the soldiers had ravaged the house and searched everywhere, the two women were allowed to sit. Amal was now wiping the tears away from her face. A moment had passed, and as quickly as they had appeared the soldiers were now gone, leaving nothing but chaos in their path.

Sarah picked up Nahrayn and began comforting her. Amal begun wiping the blood away from Sarah's face, Sarah did not feel it, but she had been bruised, one of the soldiers had hit her as he dashed into the house.

"Is this all they came for?" asked Sarah as she cozied Nahrayn and lulled her back to sleep.

"This is what they do, they don't go after the terrorists because they can't even trust the people that they were meant to protect, they only care about survival, they only care about going home with a couple of scars and some war stories to share." Amal spoke as she struggled to lift the TV and place it back on the table, but the screen had burst, smoke rising from it, there was no point in tidying anything. The *estikaan* glasses had been shattered. Amal looked at all the mess and fell to the ground overwhelmed. She went back into her room and fell asleep. Nahrayn had fallen asleep in Sarah's arms too. But Sarah stayed awake, she could not go back to sleep, not after what had happened.

For several days, Sarah and Nahrayn traversed this nameless town. Sarah's hope was dwindling; her son must have been either dead or sold in a child trafficking ring. She went around the whole town, and whoever she met, they were not prepared to talk, but when they did, they always spoke of the same perpetrator. The evil actions of the man known as Tabbar, the most feared man within the area, his reputation preceded him; he was idolized by the mad and emulated by his followers. He was capable of any act that he was requested to do, he had no limits and he had no morality.

Sarah walked with Nahrayn in the midday, she was feeling hopeless, she had gotten very little information on Tabbar, many people that she asked accused her of being a spy working for Tabbar, and those that did work for Tabbar accused her of working for the Americans. Again as she walked lost in her own thought, she heard a voice from above her.

"You're starting to become famous here," said the voice laughing.

Sarah looked up at the nearby date palm tree, and saw that same old man hanging from it.

"I suppose I am."

"Take these," said the old man as he dropped a large stem of dates to the ground. Sarah walked and picked the stem up. Nahrayn was in glee, she enjoyed pulling off the dates from the stem.

"You know everyone is talking about a strange middle aged woman, stalking and spying this town, and carrying her daughter with her everywhere she goes."

"You know perfectly why I am here and so do they," said Sarah.

"I know why you're here," said the old man as he hacked off another stem, "But they don't, not the people."

"I'm not scared, I have nothing to fear."

"They say even Tabbar has now heard of your presence."

"Does he even exist?" asked Sarah.

"You know, I have lived here for decades," said the old man placing a date in his mouth, "But I have never seen him, I have only ever seen his wrath; the destruction he leaves behind. I have only ever seen his militia, the only problem is, no one is prepared to say what he looks like... So I may have already met him, he might even be you," said the old man laughing, then he began to descend from the palm tree, slowly pushing himself down.

"If he has heard I am here, he knows why, he knows why I came here."

"He will deny everything," said the old man.

But Sarah did not care for these warnings, she had heard plenty of them, and if she had paid them attention, she would have retreated in fear back to safety, but what is a safe life without her son, what is fear without courage? So she would not budge, and when people did not answer her about Tabbar, or her son, she would ask about Nahrayn and her family.

At the end of a hard and strenuous day, Sarah returned to Amal's house. Amal had just made a huge meal and as soon as Sarah entered, she welcomed her back, kissing Nahrayn on her cheeks. Amal had grown accustomed to living alone. Opening her doors to a stranger was difficult at first, but now she felt happy and at peace; Sarah and Nahrayn became like family to her.

It was now nighttime and the moon hung up in the heavens luminously glimmering. Amal was preparing her bed; Sarah had fallen asleep on the floor following the large meal.

Chapter 6

The Eye Of Wisdom

"Sometimes things aren't what they seem," said Azkazeal, "Sometimes knowledge can cause pain."

"But knowledge is power," said Sarah, oblivious to the fact that she had left her world and come back.

"No Sarah, knowledge is restriction, wisdom, it is wisdom that is true power. Always seek wisdom, do not seek knowledge. Those that seek knowledge and lack wisdom, find corruption, they find raw power and not the truth."

"And why do you tell me this?" she asked.

"Because these are things you are meant to know."

"And how do I grow with wisdom?"

"You must search deep within yourself, you must quiet the mind, breathe and let love imbue you with patience and stoicism." Sarah listened intently, Azkazeal spoke of things that she had never heard before, and things she was never taught. She had never been told to seek wisdom; through her life people told her to seek power, to blindly follow the dogmas created by others. The responsibility of thinking for oneself, for taking one's actions into one's own hands was never given to the people of Iraq. In her land, very few did question the powers that be, and those that did, done so in silence.

"Azkazeal, I desire the power of the wise, I desire to grow and prosper from the truth and the perfection that you speak of."

"If you are ready, then I am obliged to fulfil my duty."

"And what is your duty?" she asked.

"To give you the keys to the doors of wisdom, to open your eyes," said Azkazeal. Sarah was determined to resolve these mysteries, she did not understand what Azkazeal meant but she stayed quiet, she listened. Azkazeal lowered his head placing it upon the silky ground. He closed his eyes, and spoke, "Come to me."

So Sarah took her lamp in hand and walked to Azkazeal.

"What am I to do?" she asked.

"Look into the eyes of angels, look into the eyes of demons, and look into the eyes of man."

Sarah inspected Azkazeal's forehead, his eyes closed, upon his forehead she found a parietal eye.

"What is this?"

"It is the third eye," said Azkazeal.

Sarah inspected it in awe, she looked into this eye, and as she did she felt the plane change. Waves of hot air ran through this realm, followed by a quick wave of cold and freezing air. Sarah felt her skin tickle as if a strange electric shudder had taken over.

"I cannot see anything," she said.

"It is not for you to see a thing oh Sarah. That is for the eye, it is for the eye to see you."

So she looked into this eye, and the deeper she looked, the deeper she entered its world, as if devouring her; she fell into it, finding herself in a large arid land. In awe at what she saw, she traversed this dry and lifeless land. And in the distance upon a rock, there she saw a woman sitting down, looking at her, waiting for her.

"What is this world?" she asked Azkazeal.

"This, you shall soon come to know," his voice echoed in her mind, "the eye will show you visions, they will open your heart, they will unleash your soul!"

When she had reached the woman who sat on the rock, she realized that this woman looked exactly like herself. It was like looking into a mirror; from her hair to her clothing everything was similar. However, this woman looked different; she was almost like a white shadow, her facial features eclipsed by an almost pale and pearl like complexion. The doppelganger got up from the rock and began to walk with Sarah through the arid land. No words were spoken, they simply walked together. Finally they reached an area were dead bodies lay strewn all across the land.

"Why did you bring me here?" Sarah asked the doppelganger.

"So that you may see reality."

"Reality?" Sarah asked in astonishment. The Doppelganger fell to the floor, reaching for a dead body. She squatted next to it and invited Sarah to sit next to her, "Come over here, come and look at this."

So Sarah went and sat beside her doppelganger, inspecting the dead body.

"I cannot stand this any longer," said Sarah disgusted by the foul aroma of rotting flesh, "Why am I shown these visions? Why am I brought here?"

"This is not a choice," said the doppelganger as she pulled a dead body towards her.

"I do not want to see this," said Sarah.

"Oh but you must, you must see this," responded the doppelganger, proceeding to dig her hands into the dead body, her brittle nails tunnelling and ripping the flesh. The doppelganger pushed the body away with her left hand and held tightly with the right. With force she ripped off the flesh and cradled it in her arms, she looked at it with admiration. Sarah was shaken, but she looked on as her double ripped the flesh.

"This is it," whispered the doppelganger.

"I do not want to see this, the smell is horrid," said Sarah, but the doppelganger brought forth the flesh towards her, placing it before her eyes.

"Look!" screamed the double, "Do you not see?" she continued to push the flesh before Sarah, "This is the stone of the wise!" screamed the doppelganger.

Sarah smacked the double's hand away from her. The vision petrified her, the doppelganger's voice shook her deeply.

"Smell it, this is reality," said the doppelganger.

"I do not want this anymore!" shouted Sarah.

The doppelganger proceeded to lift the piece of flesh to her nose. But Sarah pushed her away, she grabbed the doppelganger, and with force thrust her away.

The doppelganger was thrown ferociously. Falling to the floor she stared into Sarah's eyes and liquefied into the darkness. And Sarah found herself standing before Azkazeal's third eye. Azkazeal looked at her with interest.

"What did the eye see?" asked Azkazeal.

"Why? Why was I shown such a thing?"

"That I cannot tell you, the eye can only see what is within you," said Azkazeal, "Look deeper, perhaps the answer resides within," he once again lowered his head and Sarah gazed into the third eye.

This time she found herself in Amal's house, she could see her body lying on the ground asleep. She shouted to herself, wondering if she had died.

"You are not dead," Azkazeal's voice echoed through her. Sarah felt calm as Azkazeal reassured her. Inspecting the room she found the doppelganger floating by her side. A thread of light was attached to her sleeping body. This thread was tied around her waist. But the doppelganger was floating freely, not restricted.

Sarah felt free, she could see the world, and she could move through it. She could move through solid objects by thought alone. And so she flew high amongst the clouds. She flew and ascended the dark Iraqi skies like an eagle, like a phoenix, nothing could stop her. And where ever she flew the doppelganger accompanied her, the double felt like an old friend.

The star filled skies felt serene and it pleased her to feel the wind against her skin. In the distance she could see flames and men trapped in cages. The images looked real, she could tell that she was in Iraq because the desert felt familiar.

So she and the doppelganger proceeded to fly to that destination, they flew through the sky towards the chaos, they flew past the fluttering bats and through the clouds. When they had reached the caged men, they could see human beings firing weapons at each other. They committed massacres and she could see their souls departing from their bodies. She could see children crying. An outlandish anger overtook her when she witnessed the injustice.

"This is not right," said Sarah to her double, "There must be a being watching this, there must be a power watching this that will intervene." For that moment the double smiled back at her, and Sarah felt a huge presence permeate the cosmos, something was ever present, something was watching her.

Knocking was heard on the door forcing Sarah out of her slumber; in her heart a strange enigma. She sat up thinking deeply about what she had just seen. It felt real... she thought to herself. She thought about it, questioning its veracity, for the visions that she was now having were more powerful and they were now difficult to distinguish from reality. She touched her face, questioning her existence, curious whether she may still be dreaming.

Chapter 7

Vertigo

Amal answered the door, it slowly crept open, almost as if from freewill. At the door stood a strange man with dark eyes, he had a long beard and an uneasy look about him. In the distance behind him stood another man who hid behind a pick-up truck that they had parked just outside at a cross road.

Sarah heard Amal call her, so she went to the door to see what was happening and why these men had come. Amal explained to her that these men claim to know Nahrayn's family; that they would take her to her family and reunite them. Sarah looked at the long bearded man wearily, she did not trust him.

"I am glad to meet you," said the suspicious man, "We have heard about how you cared for Nahrayn, how you tried finding her family. The father is a close friend of mine, and we are very grateful for all that you've done," the man played with his beard tugging and stroking it as he spoke.

Sarah looked at Amal with concern, but Amal looked happy, she looked hopeful. For that moment Sarah did not listen to the voice that whispered to her heart. She listened to others, she listened and behaved according to the expectations of those around her. To her it felt horrible, she had followed her intuition, and it was that intuition that led her here. However, she was confused and disorientated and so she gave in to their will.

When Nahrayn was brought to the man, Nahrayn began to cry. She was confused, and the man found it difficult to hold her as she struggled in his arms.

"She will be at home with her family," he said whilst Nahrayn struggled and pushed him away. "Don't worry, they are always like this at first, but when she sees her parents she will be calmer."

Sarah looked at Nahrayn with sadness, Nahrayn had become a daughter to her and now she was about to lose her. Seeing Nahrayn cry and struggle made Sarah suspicious, she did not want to offer her up so easily.

"Give her back to me," said Sarah "I want to see her parents first, tell them to come her." But the man refused, he walked back and produced a cloth of chloroform before Nahrayn's face, Nahrayn quieted down as she fell unconscious. Sarah strode forward but stopped abruptly when the man pulled a knife and held it to Nahrayn's throat.

"She is an innocent girl," pleaded Sarah, "Give her back to me!"

Sarah and Amal looked on in fear.

"Whether you are a spy," spoke the bearded man, "This is a message that you should not forget," continued the man as he got into his truck. "Stop asking questions, go home, go and forget everything that happened." He sped off into the distance, Sarah looked on, she felt her heart plummet, she felt the sadness take over.

"I will not let this happen again, not again" spoke Sarah. Through her tears she could see the pick-up truck disappearing into the distance.

A loud explosion shook the ground. Her ears writhed with pain and a shattering headache rang through her head, but she ignored it all, she ran in the street following the pick-up truck, Amal followed her. Seeing the truck disappear into the distance made Sarah feel hopeless, but Amal was spoke to Sarah of ways to get Nahrayn back.

"We'll get her back," said Amal. In the distance the sound of explosions and gunfire rang through the streets, once more a conflict was taking place, maybe it was several gangs vying for position of a useful location, or it could have been the rebels fighting the occupying forces. The two women ignored the ominous thundering, they had now gotten used to the violence, however losing someone that they loved; they could never become accustomed to.

"I will get hold of the people who took her," said Amal as they came to a fork in the road. "I'm going to try speaking to the young man at the shop, he must know these people, and maybe we can buy her back with ransom."

But Sarah knew that neither of them had money. She did not have any money to buy back Nahrayn or to buy back Ali, but maybe there was hope, thought Sarah. Maybe the man at the shop can somehow help.

"Talk to him, I will see what I can do," said Sarah as she ran. And both women departed, each with the same goal in mind, but with different paths to walk. Sarah taking the left of the road and Amal the right. The forked road had seperated them, and ran through the desert floor like a serpent's tongue.

The stars shone bright, varnishing the sky like small lamps and leading Sarah towards an unknown path. The rush of adrenaline pumping through her veins made her ignorant of the pain she felt in her feet. She ran in the darkness, and in her heart she felt a deep aching pain, because now she not only lost her son, but also put an innocent young girl in danger. People had warned her, and she felt responsible for what had just happened to Nahrayn.

She did not know where she was running to, she was simply guessing, hoping to see the pick up truck somewhere. What they were going to do to Nahrayn was unknown to Sarah, but she knew that these must have been Tabbar's men. He must have gotten word about her. If these were Tabbar's men, then they must have also been the same people to have taken Ali, she thought to herself.

In the distance she could hear people shouting; gunfire was ringing through the street and explosions going off in the distance. She walked towards the explosions in hopes of finding clues or seeing Nahrayn. She ignored everything and walked into the belly of the beast, fearlessly.

When the adrenaline did cease and the moon did reflect enough light for her to see, she saw bodies strewn against the ground. One man lay on the ground screaming and howling. His leg was gone and a trail of blood followed his amputated limb. Sarah stood there looking at him in shock, as he grabbed his stump screamed in pain. He looked at her, she stood there dazed, confused, and the rush of blood in her head made her migraine much worse, it now drifted through her skull, causing a searing pain. Her pupils had dilated enough that she could see clearly. A foreign soldier lay close by writhing in pain, he had third degree burns, and it was difficult for her to make out the degree of damage he had sustained. The soldier got up; he was limping and speaking on a walkie-talkie.

He was sent there to die by evil men, she thought to herself, those that loved war, those blinded by greed and corruption. He reminded her of her husband at that young age, the age of rebellion and stubbornness. Except the soldier's story was different. He was forced into his position, forced by the system, forced by expectations that were ingrained into his mind. The culture of violence was so embedded in him that it became a part of his life; he became a soldier, he became a weapon.

Sarah rushed to the man with the amputated leg. The bones and flesh protruding from his limb sent a strong regurgitation, she gagged, but kept her mouth closed, grit her teeth and tried to help the man. Taking hold of her *abaya* she ripped pieces of cloth off of it and tightly tied them around the man's leg. By this time he had passed out, possibly from blood loss, possibly from pain. She lifted the man, placing him on her shoulders, she gasped, coughing profusely, but pressed on, walking, trying to find help.

She wanted to find Nahrayn, but she couldn't leave this man to die. Blood ran down her clothes, her thighs burnt with each step she took, but she gasped and pushed forward, putting each foot in front of the other. Another explosion went off nearby, sending debris flying, and cracking into Sarah's body; she gave it no notice.

Her eardrums were quacking, and she felt a sense of vertigo. Her eyes were blood red, there was tear gas in the air, she coughed and wheezed but pushed on, and with each step that she took, she felt more alive, she felt true freedom, she felt what it was to be led by her will, what it was to be led by her destiny. Flames decorated the area and the stars could no longer be seen. The flames were dancing once more, dancing and waving, flicking and gesticulating. Her clothes flickering in the wind like the flames, but now her clothes were red, red from the limb that lay against her shoulder. Her weak and old hair flew into her eyes obstructing her vision. She had heard of an old hospital within the area from Amal. And so she planned to take this man to the hospital, to talk to someone, maybe force them to give her information about Tabbar's location.

She carried the man, who to her now felt like a burden, she had no choice but to help him, but she felt saddened that she could not pursue Nahrayn's kidnappers. There were too many thoughts in her mind, too much chaos, and so she learned to absord it, to adapt to it. She chose to tackle each issue one step at a time, for if she caved in to the chaos, she would surely drown.

Suddenly a huge shadow had appeared before her, she skid against the ground sending a cloud of smoke into the air. Stopping in position captivated and shook by this huge demonic shadow. The dark figure had descended from the skies. The demon landed with a thump before her and she was overtaken by fear. The vertigo had taken its toll and she collapsed to the harsh ground, her head wrapped by the body of the unconscious man.

A light blinded her, the light was coming from the huge metallic beast that pushed the sand into the air and roared magnificently. The smoke that covered this dark shadow was now dissipating. The light of the helicopter darted around searching for any hostiles. Sarah lay on the ground, looking at it as bulky men rushed out; they came rushing to the cries of a fellow soldier. The soldier with the burns was being helped onto the helicopter, his walkie-talkie dropped to the ground as he was grabbed and aided by his fellow soldiers. Medics came out of the helicopter, a mixture of foreign and Iraqi forces.

She lay the man before them, the cloth had done little to stop the blood loss, and he was still unconscious. They rushed to get him medical attention. The blood was warm, it had covered Sarah's body and she had not noticed. It had kept her warm when she ran through the cold desert night. Lying down due to the vertigo; Sarah took a deep breath. The savage sound of explosions and gunshots could still be heard in the distance. She looked at the soldiers, all were different, they looked different, many ethnicities, many body types. She took a moment to think, she did not know where Nahrayn or her son were. The incredulity of what had just happened seeped into her consciousness, never had she done anything so brave before in her life, and done something for someone else, someone that she knew very little about...

The thundering of the AK47s woke her up from her daydream; they serenaded the night's sky invigorating it with emotion. She stumbled towards the soldiers, towards the translator.

"We are here to fight the terrorists," spoke the translator before Sarah could reach them.

"I need you to help me," she said. The men looked at her with intrigue, "I have lost my children, I need to know where they are, and I need to find them. I have lost a young boy, and I also have lost a young girl?"

The translator called to the man with the burns. The burnt soldier was being treated by medics; they were applying some form of cream to his skin and wrapping him up. Sarah saw the burns on his face, she stayed silent, but what she saw shook her, this man was not meant to be here, he was not meant to suffer this she thought to herself. The translator spoke to the man in English, and the man responded.

"He says that there are several bases in these areas, where they hold children and other people who were kidnaped. We do not know what they do with them there, they may be sold for prostitution or used for ransom," said the translator.

"Where is their main base?" asked Sarah.

"The soldier says they have many, but there is a primary one that they use for kidnapped children, it is hidden south-east of here."

"Thank him for this information."

"I know you are looking for your son, but I have a duty to stop you, you must not go anywhere near where you're heading," spoke the translator, "These are dangerous people, these are very dangerous people."

"I will not go there, but I need to know everything I can know." Sarah promised them.

"In any case" spoke the translator taking out a small mobile phone from his pocket, "Take this with you, if you see anything, or discover any new information, tell us. We have also installed a GPS device in there, if we hear any news about those terrorists, or manage anything, we will call you."

Sarah took the small mobile phone thanking the man and disappearing into the darkness of the night, she had told them she would go home, but she knew where she was going, soaked in blood, but also soaked in a mother's fury she walked the darkness, south-east. Into a world she did not understand and into an experience she will never forget. The soldiers looked on as the crimson woman dissolved into the night, her footsteps veiled by the echoing gunfire.

The translator tried to stop her, he had told her before she left, that walking alone at this time of night was illegal, it was martial law, but he bit his own tongue when he saw her eyes, her will, and her fury.

Chapter 8

A Woman In Red

The muscles in her body quivered with a dull pain. She could feel her parched throat burn with thirst. She was tired, but she gathered all of her energy and continued. The blood that once ran across her body had been warm, but now it was cold, now it was dry and thick. Her feet burnt and her muscles ached. She walked south-east, all she had was the hope, the hope that her path led her to the ones she loved.

As she walked this path, the sound of screaming and gunfire bacame more audible. However now, she no longer walked this path as a victim, no, she now walked this path as a warrior.

Eventually she could hear the gurgling sound of throats being slit. She looked from afar, and she could see a large pick-up truck similar to the one that the kidnappers used when they took Nahrayn.

Men sat on it, all holding firearms and blades. Next to them was a large ditch. Within the ditch were thousands of bodies covered in a pool of blood. There were soldiers and civilians; it was a massacre. Sarah draped herself in her crimson *abaya* and lay down in the sand trying to blend into the environment. She could see small children in the vehicle; they were blindfolded, tied, and unconscious. Like a crimson beast she crept and inspected her prey and crouching like a tiger.

The cries of sadness and despair rung through the area as each person begged and pleaded before their throat was slit. Their bodies were hurled into the ditch; a grave dug by the hands of the murderers themselves.

Lying on her stomach, she crawled towards the large pick-up truck, trying to remain hidden and veiled. As she walked closer to the truck, she could see Nahrayn in the back and Nahrayn was still unconscious. These criminals like to keep things silent, she realized, so she too must also be silent.

The terrorists were sitting around a flame, watching their friend slit throats. They were busy with their task, and by this time Sarah had managed to sneak, crawling beneath the pick-up truck.

She had searched and peered inside the truck to look for the keys, but they could not be found. So she stayed beneath it, keeping here eyes on the terrorists and watching them. They pulled out anther man's body from the truck, their feet right before her eyes, she entertained the idea of attacking at this point, to save this man's life, but she couldn't afford to risk putting Nahrayn's life in further danger. They took the man and placed a gun to his head as he lay by the ditch.

She waited, and when the terrorists were preoccupied, she stretched forth her hands from under the pick-up truck, grabbing onto Nahrayn's unconscious body. Dragging Nahrayn's body across the ground and embracing it, Sarah could feel

Nahrayn's heartbeat as she hugged her tightly. The men's roaring laughter could be heard, they were laughing at a joke that one of them had heard from a friend. Holding onto Nahrayn, Sarah began to pull herself from under the pick-up truck, slowly crawling away.

She took each breath, pacing it carefully. Deep breathing, carefully so as to not make any sound. The beads of sweat that ran down her face were like pieces of ice. When she had felt that she had moved far enough she began to crouch, and draped Nahrayn in her clothes, covering her from the cold and from the enemy's sight. Sarah started to feel Nahrayn moving, she was waking up, and when she finally awoke, she began to cry. Noticing this, Sarah began to run, but it was too late. She could hear the men shouting behind her. She could hear the pick-up truck being started. The headlights of the pick-up truck illuminating the dark, but Sarah ran, ran like she had never before in her life. The headlights were pointed directly at her, and she can see her shadow projected largely before her, mimicking her as she stabbed the cold sand with her heels, trying to push herself forward with all the might that she can muster.

Biting her lips she pressed forward, lifting her head to the skies. Trying to ignore the shadows that mirrored her; that mocked her. The engine's humming was like a predator's growl; its fearsome eyes illuminating the dark streets. A hard object cracked into the back of her skull sending her down into the darkness once again; down she descended as the howling of the terrorists' voices faded into oblivion. The fears, the anguish, all had disappeared and she stood once more at the gates of her own mind, within the darkness of her own being.

Azkazeal hovered before her, "Welcome back". She was back once again, as if she had never gone, as if reality were just a dream, merely a game. His eyes were shining strangely, and he looked different, he looked content and calm. His skin had become luminous; she could see her reflection in his now black and silvery coat.

"Not in the best of situations are you?" asked Azkazeal.

"No, but it couldn't have gone any other way."

"What have you learnt?"

"I met people, I met heartless soldiers, I met soldiers with a heart of gold, and I met the most ignorant of men."

"But what has that taught you about yourself?" asked Azkazeal.

"I learnt that I am no better than anyone else, I learnt the secret to all power," responded Sarah.

"The secret to all power?" the Serpent looked intrigued, "Do you truly think you know that?"

"The power of love," she responded.

"What of the power of love?" he asked curiously?

"It is the power to face the terrible, the power to comprehend the chaos, and the will to pursue your destiny."

"But Sarah, what of fear?"

"What about fear?"

"Fear is the enemy of love, it is the antithesis, live life in fear and you shall drown in the darkness just like my brother." Sarah sat as the Serpent spoke, "Fear of each other and fear of people's differences is what made them torture each other, it's what makes them hate each other and what makes them live a caged life. But Sarah, always remember this, that anyone can cause discord, anyone can cause chaos and savagery, but only very few people can bring men together, only a pure heart can accomplish such a feat."

A moment passed as Sarah remained sitting, contemplating the Serpent's wisdom.

"You must speak to Mazaroth," spoke Azkazeal.

"Why don't you speak to him?"

"Because only those who have ascended may pull someone out of darkness, you are such a person."

"But he is difficult," she explained.

"You must try, and after you have spoken to him, come back to me, your physical body is in deep danger, and something must be done."

With that Sarah walked towards Mazaroth, who as usual, was hovering in the distance. Upon his face was a look of melancholy.

Mazaroth turned towards her as she approached, "Who is responsible for what you see? Is it me? Or is it those in power, those that do not see the effects of their actions?"

"That's an easy question Mazaroth, you are asking who is responsible, the cause or the effect?"

"Who made them? Who made these people?"

"Do I have the answers to these questions?" asked Sarah.

Mazaroth looked away with concern, "I want all to follow an eternal creed. I want all actions to be like calligraphy, beautiful and purposeful."

"Is this what you have been thinking about whilst I was away?"

"You were not gone for long, you need to understand how time works."

"Do you want me to contemplate upon your riddles, is this how I can learn?" asked Sarah.

"What I speak of is not simply the product of contemplation. It is the product of studying history, seeing it repeat itself. And after seeing several thousand peoples, cultures and races repeat the same mistakes ad infinitum; you can come to where I am." said Mazaroth.

"Why do you let these things affect you?" she asked.

"Did you not abide and swear by the creed that Azkazeal gave? The creed that helped you see."

"That I am you and you are me..." said Sarah as if an epiphany.

"This is why I cover the truth with the darkness!" explained Mazaroth with zeal.

"I don't believe in darkness anymore," she responded

"What do you mean?" Mazaroth stretched his neck looking intrigued at Sarah, "How can you compare the two opposites, how can you deny its existence?" said Mazaroth.

"How can you accept the darkness when it can be destroyed by the light? Darkness does not exist, it is simply but a state of negativity, it is simply but a lack of light."

"Are you as audacious as to deny the darkness, what next, will you deny silence?" asked Mazaroth.

"Negative states do exist," she adjusted her argument, "As does silence, great wisdom can be found in the serenity of nothingness, and the peace of the darkness. But to be absorbed in the negativity is self-destruction."

"But the darkness existed before the light was ever conceived, the darkness is eternal always has been and always will be," said Mazaroth pugnaciously.

"But Mazaroth, what is darkness without light?" to this Mazaroth fell silent, reclining back against his sphere.

"Do not fear my dear Mazaroth, for wherever there is light, there will always be shadows, and the stronger the light, the darker the shadows."

Sarah was amazed at her versatility in this plane, her mind felt open. It was different to the world of reality. It felt as if information surrounded her, and that she could reach and utilize a wide variety of knowledge, some that she did not know before.

Mazaroth looked back at her, his voice echoing:

> *"I remember, I remember*
> *The whispering in their mind*
> *The call to war and weapons of ember*
> *I remember, I remember*
> *They avoided the darkness*
> *Afraid of what they may find*
> *I remember, I remember*
> *The man who unveiled the truth!"*

"What did this man tell them?" asked Sarah.

"He shattered the illusions, the illusion of individualism, of religion, of race, of nationalism, of languages," replied Mazaroth.

"Why did he do that?"

"To show them the creed, to help them see, that I am you and you are me!"

"And what happened to this man? Was he exalted? Is he now a legend? A myth?"

"No, Sarah. He has long been forgotten, they done what they done best, they were ignorant and they ignored him. Then fearing revolution, when the few that followed his advice had ascended, they killed him and his people."

"What was his name?" asked Sarah.

"He goes by many names, but he had no name, he was simply the manifestation of his own destiny, of his love for the truth." replied Mazaroth in a silent voice, his face that of enigmatic nostalgia.

"Sarah! You must come quickly," Azkazeal's voice echoed in the distance.

"I must go now," said Sarah to Mazaroth and he gave her a nod of acknowledgement. Sarah walked to Azkazeal. Her lamp in hand was glowing like never before, but it still was not enough to illuminate this plane, within this plane she felt like there was a vacuum, consuming all light.

"I need you to be wise when dealing with my brother," said Azkazeal, "He is intelligent, I was once his teacher, but his mind is not as it once was, it is fogged by fear, it is sullied by the actions of the past, a world now gone," said Azkazeal.

"Does he not have the right to feel so fearful, if the world will repeat its mistakes once more?"

"No Sarah, we must remain hopeful, give in to fear and all hope is lost. Your fate, my fate and that of Mazaroth's, they all are entwined. Mazaroth has yet to meet his master, and one day he shall. I will warn you Sarah, before you go back to the physical world, you must remain cautious, there is always a way, think carefully and remember the lessons that you have learned."

Her eye lids were sealed tightly. The blood that had covered them had dried, it had glued them shut. They were difficult to open. Once more she tried, she clenched them shut and again slowly pulled them open, her hands tied behind her back; it took several attempts before she could see. er vision was blurry and she experienced a burning sensation in her eyes.

When she could see; she was greeted by the vision of a dark cellar, a metallic room with no windows, it was covered with blood. She lay on the floor looking at numerous sharp objects that were thrown around from where she was. A deep throbbing pain from her neck forced her to close her eyes in agony, the throbbing continued with each heartbeat. Around her were three other people, their moaning and murmuring resonated within the small room, adding a strange ambience.

All of them were tied up and they lay on the floor next to her, manoeuvring her body; Sarah tried to get a good look at the others. On her left was a young Iraqi boy, his dark hair filled with sand, his slim and weak body pressed against a wall. He sat there, his face emotionless. To her right was a European man, he sobbed to himself, trying to make very little noise. The European's clothing was modern, he had various journalistic paraphernalia, his face and eyes were red, probably from what he's had to endure, Sarah thought to herself. After all, she had no idea how long these people have been held captive.

In the corner of the room, lay a middle aged man bleeding from his head, a pool of blood had collected beneath his fractured skull. The blood colouring his grey hair in ruby; he looked like he was in his late fifties, and he looked like a family man.

Regardless of where these people were, and where they came from, now they all had something in common, they were all helpless, powerless, and afraid. They waited for the unexpected, the only hope they had, was of a peaceful death, and even that seemed to them as a distant fantasy.

"Where am I, who brought me here?" whispered Sarah, she turned to the people surrounding her, but none responded. She gave another look to the people around her; the young Iraqi boy gave her a cold and dead stare.

"We were all brought here for the same reason, by the same people," said the Iraqi boy. Sarah looked at the boy as he took a moment to compose himself. He withheld his tears, tears provoked by the thoughts of his imminent demise, "We are worth more to them dead, then we are alive."

"Why us? Why have they taken us?" interjected the journalist as he struggled trying to wipe his tears away with his shoulders.

"Why they brought me here... They wanted money, and my family can't afford the ransom," said the Iraqi boy.

Sarah and the Iraqi boy looked at the journalist, and they didn't need to ask him why or how he was kidnaped. It was clear that having a foreign journalist was profitable to the terrorists. He could be used as leverage against the Iraqi government, he could be used to obtain notoriety around the world, all it took was to decapitate him and put it up on the internet.

"Why are you here?" the young boy asked Sarah.

"I came to get my son."

"If they are the ones that caught him, he is long gone. They have strong ties to the child trafficking industry," the young boy spoke the cold hard truth about this militia. Is this what Ali had to endure, she thought to herself, is this what Nahrayn has to endure?

"We are going to die, we are going to be online for everyone to see," whimpered the journalist, "They will all watch us suffer but they won't be able to help us... Maybe we can convince them to make it quick and painless, maybe we can convince them to give us pills to swallow?" the journalist spoke to himself, hopeful of a pleasant death. But his wishful thinking and his fantasies weren't taken seriously by the others.

"The man that lies there," the Iraqi boy spoke about the old man that lay in the corner of the room, "He is a family man, we spoke to him before they finally decided to get him, he thought his money was going to give him his freedom. He was almost certain of escaping, but even he couldn't".

The group looked at him, "How long has he been like this?" asked Sarah.

"He has been like this for the past thirty minutes. He begged them, he offered them his fortune but they still struck him. They didn't bring him here for money. They brought him here for revenge... So tell me again, why did they bring you here?"

"I don't know..." responded Sarah.

Several minutes passed as the captives sat in silence, and even though they were not alone, they knew that nothing they could say could change anything. The minutes felt like days and the hours like years, time had stopped. Each of them looked at their lives. They questioned themselves, what had they left behind, what was their legacy? Sarah thought about Nahrayn and Ali, she remembered her husband.

Sarah squirmed, pushing her hands against the rope that tightly tugged against her wrists. It was tied well, and each time she tried to separate them, the knot grew stronger.

"Maybe there's a way we can break these ties," whispered Sarah to the others.

"And then what? How do we leave, they'll see us, we are in the middle of nowhere," replied the young boy.

"They have guns..." added the journalist.

"We have to try" explained Sarah.

"Maybe we can try becoming their friends!" interrupted the journalist, "Maybe they'll let us out," Sarah and the young boy looked at the journalist with a look of concern, and it took a moment for him to realize how unlikely such a thing was.

"Have you found out whether they are *Sunni* or *Shiite*?" asked Sarah.

"It makes no difference, these people don't worship God, they worship power and they worship wealth," said the boy, "I've been here for a couple of days, I've seen men come and go, Jews, Muslims, Christians, and Atheists. All begged, all believed whatever they were told to believe, and yet, all ended the same. These people are not normal, their childhood, their lives, it has destroyed them."

Sarah continued struggling, pushing her body against the ground, she squirmed and wriggled. She pushed herself up against the wall to sit up so that she may understand this new environment. Meanwhile the young iraqi boy did not pay her any attention, he simply sat there in fear, staring at the blood smeared wall.

The Iraqi boy watched as Sarah struggled with the ropes, he slowly grew with agitation, "Did you even think that they would care, they cut people's heads off, they actually take someone's head off! A living person's head and cut it off whilst he begs, whilst he prepares himself for the pain. These aren't the brain washed suicide bombers, these are the commanders..." With that the young boy's ominous speech resonated in the heads of the other captives; the fear was contagious, forcing them to sit and wait in silence.

They looked at the room; each smear of blood spoke of a different person, what they had experienced, a tale now forgotten. The walls were

clawed leaving marks and scratches across them.
Each scratch on the wall was an experience that
someone had to live through, their last seconds on
earth; a living hell.

Chapter 9

An Esoteric Silence

"Sarah, my name is Sarah... I am a widow
looking for her son. I am a mother who lost
a daughter. I want to be remembered by those

chosen by the universe, those that the universe chose to die by my side." The young Iraqi boy and the journalist looked at her in silence, confused.

"I am Ramy," spoke the young boy, "I am only a student, my family are well known throughout our neighbourhood, but our reputation was all built with lies, we were not rich, nor were we powerful. They captured me as I went to university in Baghdad, I was studying medicine. But the ransom that they requested... my family couldn't afford it."

"My name is Alexander," spoke the journalist, "I am a private investigator. They warned me about coming here, but I didn't listen, I couldn't listen, I wanted to see the world; I wanted to change the world. I thought I would find the stories that would touch people's hearts. That would maybe change their views on war, but, I myself will now become a story, one that'll be forgotten and lost."

Lastly the group looked at the man that lay in the pool of his own blood.

"I will speak for him," said Ramy, "We will always remember him, his tale will not be forgotten, a faithful family man. When I spoke to him he was always hopeful. His name is Rashid."

The comfort they gained from this was enough to quiet their minds; the reciprocal emotions that they felt helped them accept what had happened. Each had their own story, but now they knew that even in their last dying moment, atleast their names would be remembered, they would at least be loved. The bonds they had created, they knew the bonds would not last, they knew that when they lose each other, the bonds would be shattered, the sadness would be unbearable. But, they also knew that in each other's dying moment, the last thing that they see of this world, won't be empty cruelty, and they knew that they wouldn't die lonely.

The ominous noise of clanging metal sounded from outside the room. The humming of an engine bellowed through the hallways as the terrorists approached, their roars of laughter forcing the captives to shiver in fear. On the wall of the room were hung several knives and other torture equipment, some were still unused, shining and clean, whilst others had rusted, sheathed in a layer of dried blood. Alexander had managed to block these items out from his mind, he simply lay lost in his own fantasies; daydreams of being back home; living his then mundane life.

The door to the room was sent swinging, cracking against the concrete wall. The light bulb swayed in the darkroom sending shadows darting and quivering. The terrorists entered, they were average looking men, some had their faces covered. A small man of short stature walked behind them holding a cheap looking camcorder and tripod.

Sarah was amazed, that these average looking men, were the ones behind what she saw in the dark night, the ones that sat by the pick-up truck. The illusion that they had created was no more, now that she could clearly see their faces.

Upon their faces was a look of emptiness. Very few of them smiled, but those that did, had a look in their eyes, as if they were suffocating. Their fists tightly clenched, an armour to protect them from their past, a past filled with fear, filled with torture and a lack of attention. Now, they were making up for it, they were the beasts, they were the ones causing the destruction. Some of them looked at the captives with zeal, proud of what they had accomplished. They had risen to power with malice and raw force, a relentless and merciless philosophy.

They walked over Rashid's unconscious body, Ramy looked away, and Alexander stared in fear. They could do nothing but watch. Sarah was snaring at the terrorists, angry and furious, these were the people who had taken her son. These were the people that had taken Nahrayn, stolen her from a new loving mother. These were the people that had desecrated a once sacred land, once an advent for knowledge, now but a place of savagery and fear.

There were approximately ten men who had walked in, they noted Sarah's stare and saw the fear in Alexander's body. The terrorists walked over to them, looking down upon them, standing high as if gods. They were calm inspecting Alexander with an almost strange serenity.

"Don't be afraid," spoke one of the men to Alexander, "Things aren't what they look like."

To this Alexander returned a weak and innocent smile, looking up to them, as if a dog hoping to appease his owners. They looked at each other, and with sinister smiles, looked back down at Alexander. They kicked him several times, his skull bouncing off the floor as he whimpered. Sarah was shaken, gasping in horror at what they were doing.

"And what's wrong with your eyes?" questioned one of the men as he pummelled Sarah in the stomach, she wheezed trying to catch her breath.

Ramy begged them to stop, but they ignored him celebrating with cackles of glee like hyenas. Sarah knew there was no point in begging for mercy, if they had gone this far and caused so much destruction, why would they stop now? Especially considering the amount of victims that must have begged and pleaded. She knew that they weren't the first.

To the terrorists the captives were business, they were work, and to others they were a form of entertainment. They enjoyed violating all notions of morality and ethics. They enjoyed putting others through the same pain and fear that they felt inside themselves.

One of the men attached a small blade to his shoe; he practised kicking the air, making sure it doesn't slip off.

"What are you doing? Take that off and stop being stupid!" the short man shouted at him; with that the short man continued fiddling with the tripod and camcorder, he was busy trying to figure out how to use it.

Sarah noted that very few of them had Iraqi dialects. They had accents ranging from a variety of places. A few of the men looked very young, as if in their late teens. They were somehow brainwashed into coming her, their violent actions paid with money and respect, things these men may have never experienced in their lives. They must have lived vacant existences, but now they experienced praise, and they experienced attention. The terrorists gathered around Sarah, like beasts, they eyed her.

"We can have a lot of fun with this one," said one of the men as he caressed Sarah's body.

"Not now!" shouted the short man with agitation, as he tried to use his new and unfamiliar equipment. The others looked at the short man with fear, they moved away from Sarah, as they sleazily eyed her.

"So how much is each worth?" asked one of the terrorists.

"We should just take the ransom, it is easy money," interrupted another.

"No," spoke the short man in frustration, "We do both, ransom and the other." On hearing this Alexander let out a gasp of shock. The terrorist who had taken the blade off his shoe picked it up once more. He grabbed Alexander, pulling him by the hair, and placed the blade firmly in Alexander's mouth. The terrorist looked at Alexander, pushing his jaw up against the blade. The sharp metallic taste permeated through Alexander's being as he squirmed and hummed with fear.

"Say something," the terrorist pressed, "Say something, say anything." The short man noticed what was happening.

"What are you doing?" asked the short man, the room went quiet. The terrorist ratracted the blade out from Alexander's mouth. Alexander spat the blood to the side, choking and coughing.

"You don't do anything without my permission, you don't do anything like that again to someone as valuable as him! Do you understand?" The terrorist did not respond, being scolded so harshly before the others hurt his pride. He cleaned the blade with a cloth as he eyed the short man with a look of a disobedient dog.

"Don't look at me like that," said the short man, "He is worth more money than you think; he is worth more than you. Stop fucking with my plan!"

The silence continued, and in this silence all that could be heard was the plastic clicking of the camcorder, the bleeping of the machine and clanking of the metal pieces. The militia sat in silence as they watched their leader.

"Tabbar?" spoke one of the men to the short man.

"Yes?" replied the short man.

Sarah looked at him in amazement, this was the famed Tabbar, this was the man who had created so much destruction, this was the man who had terrorised and murdered thousands of people, and this was the man who owned millions in wealth.

"What do we do about the kid?"

"That does remind me..." said Tabbar as he walked towards Sarah and knelt. "What is that child to you? Is she your daughter?"

Sarah looked back at Tabbar, her heat beating. She had lost those eyes of fury that she had, and she was no longer gambling with her life, in her hands rested Nahrayn's fate.

"What difference does it make?" asked Sarah.

"What is she to you? Why did you risk your life for her?"

"She is me, I am her," she said, but the men laughed at Sarah.

"Maybe she is crazy, look at her covered with blood," spoke one of the men. "She probably kidnaps children to kill them herself, she does not look right."

"Are you a cannibal?" asked Tabbar mockingly.

"You stare into my eyes and ask me such a question? You too also once had a mother. Do you not understand why I do and say what I say?" Tabbar looked at her perplexed, and eyed her spitefully.

"You know, I've spoken to many captives, but none have spoken like you. Why is that?" Sarah looked away in silence averting her eyes. "Sell the kid," said Tabbar to his associates as he returned to the camcorder.

"What about him?" one of the men pointed at Rashid's cracked head.

"The client gave as promised, we have to fulfil our end of the deal," replied Tabbar. By now some of the men had left the room. Tabbar remained in the room and continued setting the camcorder up, fiddling through several tapes. Next to the door another terrorist sat on a rusty metal chair, rocking it back and forth, he kept his gaze pointed at the captives. The rusted metal chair squealed with each movement.

"I was told to come and see you" spoke a young boy from the door with a strange dialect. He had a peculiar face, he looked very young but he had a very long beard and a shaved moustache.

"Yes I wanted to show you our work, our struggle," said Tabbar as he welcomed him in. Tabbar proceeded to show the boy Sarah and the others, he lifted Rashid's head, pulling it up from the floor by his hair. Tabbar spoke to the young boy about paradise, he spoke about Sarah and the others, calling them *Shayateen*. He told him of how these people were of the devil, that they had missed the grace of God and how they were now the victims of their own actions.

"One day you will commit the ultimate sacrifice, you will fall and in your place flames will rise, they will feel your wrath, and your place in paradise will be secured," said Tabbar to the boy.

"We are not the *Shayateen*, we have not hurt anyone," spoke Sarah, "How do you expect to enter paradise with these actions?"

"Do you see how they seek to mislead you?" spoke Tabbar, "Here take these," Tabbar took some strange capsules out of his pocket. He counted them, separated them in groups and passed several of the capsules to the young boy. The boy took them and swallowed them without any water.

"There are spiritual masters," the young boy said to Sarah. "I take their advice, just as I take the advice of professionals in any other field." Tabbar lead him out of the room, speaking to him of the afterlife that the young terrorist would attain, the suffering and torture of the others who did not believe him.

Tabbar spoke to him of bodily pleasures, of ideal beauties in heaven. Heaven, was, according to Tabbar, a hedonistic and egocentric dream, a paradise where only the ego matters. He spoke of hell, an eternal place of torture and death, a place with no mercy. Tabbar assured the young boy that a large sum of money was being prepared to care for his family after he completed his mission. The young boy was lead out of the room; he left the room as if in a stupor. Soon everyone had left this cell, all that remained were the captives and the guard that continued to rock on the rusted metal chair.

The man that sat in the rusty chair remained; he continued to look at Sarah blankly, emotionless.

The captives sat in silence, a few hours passed. All the men were armed, and the captives knew that their fight was a futile one. But Sarah watched, she studied the people around her, she studied this new devilish environment. She took note of everything. Being placed into such a predicament, Sarah was forced to think on her feet. She sat for those several hours calculating, creating inferences and taking note of everyone's personality.

Alexander and Ramy didn't cry or beg anymore, the fatigue had left them tired and weary. They had tried various things, and none had worked. Keeping silent, they thought, may buy them more time; it may help make the process easier, there was nothing that wasn't said or anything that could be said. Several failures confirmed to them that; speaking to these people will change nothing, their mind was a crystallized mind. These people had gained experience, they knew how to block out the begging and pleading that accompanied much of their work.

After several hours, the terrorists came back, entering the cell. All of them had their faces covered this time. Tabbar came in after them carrying a huge plastic mat.

"Who's going to take this one?" asked one of the masked men.

"Give it to the new guy," replied Tabbar as he proceeded to place the huge mat on the floor, stretching it before the camcorder. They dragged Rashid's still unconscious body over the mat. They gathered around the camcorder, some of them placed banners affiliating themselves with various groups and various creeds. One of the men knelt behind Rashid's unconscious body holding a rusty short blade. Tabbar ordered the men, making them stand around Rashid in an orderly manner. They made sure that his face was well covered, one of them held a piece of cardboard behind the camcorder; a long speech written on it.

"Has it been done?" a foreign voice enquired from outside the room. Tabbar left the room, the masked men looked on, waiting for Tabbar to return. Clearly there was someone higher than Tabbar, someone that Tabbar had to answer to. Sarah noted that Tabbar did not operate completely out of his own freedom and choice.

"It's nearly done, are you sure you want him?" Tabbar's voice could be heard outside.

"Just do what you're told," spoke the voice arrogantly.

"Of course..." replied Tabbar in a hushed voice.

"I want the world to see this," said the foreigner as his footsteps faded into the distance. Tabbar returned to the room looking frustrated.

"Come on, let's start!" spoke Tabbar as he adjusted the camcorder. The masked men had lined up behind Rashid, the executioner was young, and he was chosen so that he may climb through the ranks of this new cult that he had joined.

The executioner began to talk to the camcorder, his eyes pointed straight at the lens. He proclaimed how those that have gone against them shall perish, he spoke of an unrealistic ideal; one that was marred by ignorance and enforced by barbarism.

"Our enemies, the enemies of our religion, the enemies of our people, they will feel this blade! Just as we have felt the blade of their oppression!" savagely shouted the executioner.

At that moment, Rashid's eyes opened wide, and he moaned with pain. His head was sore and his wound was still open, lightly dripping blood. The wound had a rotten green tinge to it; it was infected.

The commotion around him had awakened him from his unconventional slumber. He looked at the man with the blade and wept with fear like a child, the executioner looked at him in shock, and the blade dropped out from his hand. The blade's clanging against the blood stained concrete rang through the room, sending it into a silence whilst the executioner looked at the camera in fear.

"Do it, pick it up!" shouted Tabbar. The executioner lifted the rusty blade hastily in an attempt to overcome his rationality. The masked men chanted religious slogans as they grabbed hold of Rashid's limbs holding him down like a lamb. The executioner pressed his knee against Rashid's upper back. He grabbed Rashid from his hair. Rashid felt his hair being pried away; he could hear his now blood covered hair crackle and rip away from his dented cranium.

"I have children!" whimpered Rashid as he looked up at the executioner teary eyed.

"Kill him!" shouted Tabbar heatedly. At that moment Sarah fell unconscious, what she was seeing shook her, it disgusted her and she could not bear it any longer. Her weak body and the stress she had endured, as well as the thoughts that raced through her mind had destroyed her internally.

"I have a family, please I offer everything, my soul, my money, everything, don't do this to me... don't do this to them!" said Rashid in an attempt to avoid his ever looming death.

"Do it!" shouted Tabbar once more, at that moment; the executioner's *keffiyeh* that once covered his face fell off; showing the executioner's face to the camcorder. Tabbar switched the camcorder off as he looked at the executioner furiously.

"This was meant to be a message, this was meant to be a symbol of our power, our rage..." said Tabbar. The executioner looked at Rashid in sadness; Rashid took a few breaths of relief. Tabbar was angry, he had an arrangement and things did not go as planned. He told the executioner to sit and keep his eyes on Sarah and the others; to watch them whilst he takes care of business. They dragged Rashid outside.

"We had a deal, we agreed that it would be a message, a strong message," the foreign voice could be heard once more from outside the room.

"I'm sorry, we have to commit to another plan," spoke Tabbar in sadness.

"This is not sufficient; you told us that this could be fixed, that this would benefit all of us," spoke the voice.

Rashid could now be heard begging and pleading, screaming in fear. A gunshot rang through the small room, leaving Ramy and Alexander in terror.

"It can be fixed," said Tabbar, "They won't be able to tell the difference... Get the blade!"

Chapter 10

A Fire That Consumes None

Sarah looked around her, the darkness that she had grown accustomed to was no longer there, and Azkazeal had a strange luminosity to him. Upon Azkazeal's skin were many patterns and beautiful calligraphy. Around her were trees, beautiful and colourful flowers, that now decorated the once dark and gloomy ground. The beautiful scent of roses and honey perfumed the air in this world. Fireflies surrounded her, attracted to her as if she were a light bulb.

Behind her, in the distance, Mazaroth was looking at her. He hung in the air; he however seemed darker than ever before, he hung in the sky as if a silhouette.

"Welcome Oh ascended master," Azkazeal spoke in a soft voice, he humbly bowed before Sarah as if in prostration. "I am under your command," said Azkazeal, fireflies were floating around him attracted to his luminous skin.

"What does this mean?" asked Sarah in amazement. His voice had changed dramatically; it now soothed her, touching her heart, bringing her closer to an ineffable truth. It reminded her of her mother's voice, the voice that once sang her to sleep.

"You need not worry my dear, all shall be in sight, just be patient. I brought you hear to tell you something that you were decreed to hear, something you were decreed to comprehend and spread."

"And what is it? Oh Azkazeal?" asked Sarah.

"That to fear death, is to fear life," said Azkazeal.

"But death, it torments me, it torments all living things."

"Always remember that death for some is mercy," he said.

"The people that I have seen in my life were not merely afraid of death, they are afraid of pain, a painful death, one filled with torture." she explained.

"Torture is always self-inflicted, Sarah you must remember, you are not capable of hurting others; no human is."

"What about the things that I am seeing happening before me, the crooks the criminals, even governments are doing it, are they not hurting others?" asked Sarah.

"They hurt others in the short term, but the physical heals, most wounds heal; the wise grow stronger. But, he who commits these atrocities, is left with wounds upon their souls, something that penetrates and escapes the bounds of reality and consciousness, these wounds my dear, do not always heal," responded Azkazeal.

"What about vengeance?" asked Sarah as she picked up a luminous flower from the ground and smelled its sweet perfume.

"Vengeance may sate your thirst for blood, but it cannot heal the wounds, it only conceals the symptoms. Descend into the darkness to find the hidden light, but do not let it consume you."

"I understand what you mean, when man tortures man a part of him dies, a part of him wallows in darkness. But there must be vengeance; there must be justice in this world!" said Sarah.

"Yes Sarah, justice, not excessive brutality. Vengeance is a dangerous fire, tame it and do not let it scorch or engulf you."

"So what am I to do?" she asked.

"You do what feels right, you do what you must. I cannot give you the answers to these things, these are things you must discover on your own, I can only help guide you as you help guide me. So you must transform Sarah, you must find a way to transmute all the negativity into the positive, you must escape the shackles. Have no fear, have no fear."

"But many of us are simply the product of our governments, the rulers that enforce their ideologies."

"Then that is who you must affect, that is who your message will reach and torment; the instigators, the rulers, those that pull the strings." said Azkazeal.

"I will do what I can, if the cosmos wills it."

"You must speak to Mazaroth, he has been waiting for you," said Azkazeal, Sarah looked at Mazaroth. She began to walk to him but she was duly stopped by Azkazeal, "Do not forget your lamp."

"I do not need it any longer, I can now see this world."

"You will need it for Mazaroth," he explained.

So Sarah picked up the lamp and held it tightly as she walked to Mazaroth. And as she walked, the darker it got, as if descending into a dark ocean. From where she stood, Azkazeal seemed like a shining silhouette of light. As she approached Mazaroth, he tried to avert his eye, trying to look away.

"I see that you still cling to your sphere?" said Sarah as Mazaroth looked away into the dark abyss. "Do you not see the light that now warms us? Do you not see how we have grown?" sha asked.

"I am sorry, oh Sarah, I am truly sorry!" apologized Mazaroth as Sarah looked at him puzzled. The sphere that he had coiled slowly began descending till it was falling at a ferocious velocity, it descended as if it were being dragged by an invisible force. It landed slamming the dark ground like steel crashing against steel, and now he was face to face with Sarah.

Seeing Mazaroth so close, Sarah realized that he looked like Azkazeal when she first met him. He had dark skin like a black mamba, devouring all light that came upon it.

Mazaroth began to let go of his sphere; uncoiling from it, he stood atop it in a striking position, poised and hissing. Sarah looked at the sphere, in confusion; it was nothing but another egg. Sarah was shocked, she had thought that Mazaroth had encapsulated the sun, but he did not, he held something different.

"Is this what you call the truth?" asked Sarah. Mazaroth looked upset and dazed.

"I am no longer of any use to you oh ascended one, let me be, let me wallow in my own darkness. Your eyes, they could see, they could peer through the darkness, and yet you uncovered all, no stone was left unturned. You stood staring at a lie, when the truth was within you from the start."

"What do you mean Mazaroth?"

"The truth was nothing but the savage manifestation created by the hands of man, it dwelt within him, but it was perverted, it was destroyed. But you stood fearlessly; you peered into the darkness knowing well what lay within, and with wisdom, your discerning eye pierced through the evil to find the inner light. You have ascended and yet my master wallows in fear."

Sarah did not know how to react, Mazaroth was kind, but he had lied to her, he had deceived her, all to protect his ego and to protect his master. Mazaroth did not have the light to this world, neither was he shielding a sun, he was but the guardian of another person's destiny.

"If I have found the light within my darkness, than I shall help you find the light within yours," said Sarah.

"Only my master could do such a thing," he replied.

"Then I shall guide your master, if it is my destiny, then my actions will resonate through the cosmos, and affect those that were decreed to be guided."

"But I have deceived you oh Sarah, the pain in my heart, it is too much to bear," sulked Mazaroth.

"You did what you thought it was best to do, but now you see the truth, and it shall guide you."

Mazaroth looked at her, touched by her words.

He coiled once more around his sphere, upon his face a look of serenity. She bid him farewell and walked back once more to Azkazeal.

"There is not much I can teach you," said Azkazeal to Sarah, "But there is more for you to teach me, refine my soul, and I shall refine yours."

"I must go back," said Sarah looking sad.

"Do not fear, I will watch over you," said Azkazeal as Sarah awoke dazed. In front of her was Alexander lying on the floor, an empty expression upon his face, he saw her awaken, and spoke with a monotonous voice, "We must accept the end, there is no escape, there is no hope."

Ramy was not in the room, and so she looked around, curious as to what might of happened to him. The only other person in the room with them was the executioner that had failed Tabbar. He sat at the entrance holding his head in regret.

"Where is Ramy?" asked Sarah.

"They took him. They just took him without explaining what they were going to do to him. They're going to kill me anyway; they are going to bargain with me, they are going to showcase me."

"Stay calm" whispered Sarah.

"Calm?" asked Alexander sarcastically.

All the while the man at the entrance watched them, and listened. Sarah looked at him, and whispered in a hushed voice, "I want to talk to you". The man got up and walked over to Sarah, he was still angry from what had happened, he had lost his rank and had been vilified. He walked over to Sarah kneeling next to her as she whispered to him.

"You don't want to do this," she said, but the man did not respond, he simply got back up and as he was walking away, "Wait!" Sarah shouted, "You do not want to be here, you do not want to do this, I can see it in your face, I can see it in your eyes, and I can hear it in your voice."

The man stopped, he looked back at Sarah, his hand tightly holding his rusted blade, as he unsheathed it; pulling it away from his holster.

"Do you know who these people are?" said the executioner, "Do you know what they can do to my family, to my tribe?"

"I know, I know it too well. But do they know what you're capable of? Do they know what you can do?" asked Sarah.

"No, they underestimate me; they judge people on their heartlessness, not on their skills. Nothing can be changed, it's all over, they are going to do something to me soon, they don't trust me anymore."

"There is still time to change all of this, there is still time. You can make the world what you want it to be."

The executioner walked back over to Sarah, he held the knife tightly as he hovered over Sarah, the rusted blade looking dull with a ravenous appetite for blood. Alexander cowered into the corner trying to shield his eyes from what was going to happen.

"Please don't hurt her," he said. But Sarah did not flinch, her reaction was one of determination, the executioner knelt next to her, and began to cut the thick ropes that had held her hands so tightly.

"If you want to leave, you must do so now. They are outside somewhere, they left me here to watch over you, but they underestimated me," said the executioner as he cut the rope.

"What about Ramy?" asked Alexander.

"He's being recruited," answered the executioner. Alexander and Sarah looked at each other with concern; the thought that he was coerced into working with such nefarious people was understandable. Under threat of death, most people would do anything. The terrorists would probably need someone like him too; someone with some medical knowledge would come in handy in the battlefield. Perhaps the thought that his family would be safe was what really obligated Ramy to make such a decision.

"Everyone's left?" asked Alexander. The executioner did not reply. "Is this place empty?" again Alexander enquired.

"No, not completely," responded the executioner, "Tabbar has stayed behind to watch over the place, he's probably outside on guard."

Sarah and Alexander got up wiping their now bruised wrists. The executioner dashed to the room entrance, he slid to the side of the door, inspecting the area and pressing his back against the wall. He gestured for Sarah and Alexander to follow him. They navigated through the underground corridors, like silent mice, they moved ducking and weaving any security cameras. At last they reached a fork in the corridor, "The exit is this way," said the executioner pointing to the left, but Sarah did not move.

"Come on!" said Alexander as he tugged on Sarah.

"No, I can't..." she said.

"You must leave now, it's dangerous, if they see us, then they will kill us."

"I came to look for my son, I came for Nahrayn. I won't leave without them," said Sarah. The executioner understood what Sarah desired. So when he saw Sarah so vehement in standing her ground, he had no choice.

"They keep the prisoners through there, in a small cellar," said the executioner pointing to the right. "I'm going to find Tabbar and guard the entrance till you come back. Hurry."

Alexander did not leave Sarah's side, he accompanied her. Alexander and Sarah followed the corridor to the right, it was dark, it was hot and there was no ventilation. Sarah gasped for air as she ran. The blistering heat and strange toxic fumes that filled the corridors caused confusion. The smell of seared flesh and strange chemical compounds made Sarah and Alexander choke and wheeze. The light bulbs that hung from the ceiling swung viciously and the shadows danced in a strange magnificence.

The deeper that they went through the corridor the darker and the hotter and the worse it got. Eventually it started to cool, till they felt a cool breeze of air slam against their skin, sending chills through their bones and forcing the hairs on their bodies to stand. Loud bangs of gunfire echoed from where the executioner had ran.

Eventually Sarah and Alexander had reached a cold room, and inside this room they could see several air conditioning units humming away. They could hear the sound of a TV; it was switched on a news channel. Voices of several politicians discussing the implications of kidnappers was heard coming from the TV, they spoke of how it affected the general populace.

A large growling echoed from within the room. Sarah and Alexander approached it slowly. The growling continued; it sounded like a warning one would hear given off by wild beasts. They stopped in their spots looking at each other with tension. They walked carefully, sneaking to where the bellowing roar came from. It was Tabbar who sat on an office chair fast asleep, his chin up, his face pointed at the ceiling, his jaw hung down. His left eye, half open it seemed as if he were watching them. He however, was fast asleep. The humming of the air conditioning unit had lulled him to sleep, and provided an ambience soothing his rigid and cold nerves. Across from where he slept was a table; on it were several blades and an automatic rifle.

Next to him was a staircase leading downstairs, Sarah looked at it, she knew that this must be where they were keeping the children. She gestured to Alexander, pointing at the staircase, and so they both crept towards it. Tabbar was fast asleep, but with each snore that he took, a shiver would run up Alexander and Sarah's spine. They had to keep silent, but Tabbar's eye perturbed them; they felt like it followed them. Alexander looked at Tabbar's left eye. It was quacking with each snore, shaking and vibrating violently.

These rapid eye movements made Tabbar look as if he was awake, like a wolf he watched them approach the stairs. They stared at the eye in fear as it tormented them.

Suddenly the snoring stopped, Tabbar's mouth closed shut, his head twisted and turned and his eyes lay gaze upon them, he sat there looking at them with confusion. When the shock of his awakening had ceased, Sarah dashed to the table, Tabbar jumped to the table too. What might have been several seconds felt like an eternity to Sarah, she saw Tabbar grabbing the rifle and landing to the floor. She knew it didn't have to be over, she knew that this was not what was meant to happen. In her heart, she felt calm, she knew what she had to do, she had to believe in herself, believe in the power and wisdom of her own heart, to let go of all the fear and embrace death.

Alexander stood there in shock, frozen into his position, it all happened too quickly for Alexander. He was not used to such adrenaline filled situations. He was an intelligent man, but he had often hidden behind cameras, behind words.

Tabbar held the rifle, aiming it at Alexander and Sarah, it began to fire blazing shards of metal that would tear flesh. Sarah leapt atop Tabbar pushing the gun away and pushing Tabbar's small body down to the ground. Tabbar pulled the trigger blindly, he had a fury in his eyes, he did not like being controlled, and he especially did not like being outsmarted by a woman.

Several bullets thundered through Sarah, sending jolts of pain through her body like bolts of lightning. She pushed the rifle to the side as it fired through the tender flesh of her palm. Alexander had regained his composure, and dove at Tabbar, pushing his body down and skewing the trajectory of the bullets. Sarah and Alexander pushed Tabbar down together. They struggled with all their strength, forcing his head and chest down with their body weight.

Tabbar thrashed about trying to escape their grip; he thrashed on the floor like a fish struggling for air. The gun fired away as they both struggled to keep Tabbar under control. Bullets flew through the TV, it shattered it; smoke rising from the broken screen. The audio from the TV had ceased and a silence submerged the room, all that could be heard was the panting of Tabbar as he struggled for control.

"Take it!" shouted Sarah to Alexander, blood dripping from her mouth, "Just take it!"

Alexander made sure to hold Tabbar down well, and pried the rifle from his fingers, he held the rifle against Tabbar's head, but Tabbar did not quit.

"I'm going to kill you!" shouted Tabbar; he was more enraged than ever, he shouted as he pushed Alexander and Sarah away. But Sarah threw her body atop his once more.

Alexander took a few steps away from the mayhem, in his hand the rifle quivering, trembling with fear. In his hands he was holding a weapon, it was not in his nature to kill, and it was not something he ever thought of doing.

"I will shoot!" shouted Alexander hopelessly.

"Kill him!" spoke Sarah as blood spurted from her mouth.

Alexander took a deep breath, and aiming the rifle at Tabbar. Sarah rolled herself away from Tabbar's body leaving him exposed as he shielded himself with his forearms, cringing in fear.

Tabbar's body shook with the hail of bullets that pierced his flesh, his vital organs bursting with blood; he felt his body fill with the scorching pain of the hot lead. The rain of bullets did not cease until the clip finished, and Alexander was left looking through the smoke that emanated from the tip of the rifle, rising up like a Serpent.

He looked at Tabbar's body in shock, amazed at what he had done, the rifle dropped from his hands.

"I killed him... I killed him, with my own hands, I killed a man..." whispered Alexander in shock and fear. Tabbar's half open eye was pointed at Alexander, now nothing but a cadaver, nothing but an empty vessel. To look a man in his eyes and watch him die, that was something that hurt Alexander greatly. He wished he could have undone what he had done. But it was now too late, Tabbar was dead, and so was his reign. Alexander wiped the tears from his eyes.

"Sarah! Sarah, he is dead!" but Sarah did not respond, she lay there on the floor, she had lost too much blood. Alexander ran to her body, checking her pulse. He took a few moments to compose himself. Sarah was hurt and he was worried about her, but he knew that fear in this situation would be meaningless and decided to continue, never giving up hope. He had a prediliction to uncover the truth, and he never left a stone unturned. So he checked Tabbar's pockets; finding multiple documents ranging from contracts, to licenses and a notebook. Alexander took everything that he was able to carry with him. He checked Tabbar's shirt pocket and found some keys.

He got up once more and descended the dark stairway. The heat once more became unbearable, the air conditioning could not reach these dark underground rooms, the stench of the place forced Alexander to choke and cough. He began to breathe through his mouth attempting to escape the stench of these caverns. The lower he descended, the more audible the voices became. When he had reached the bottom, he found a room with multiple cages all filled with children of different ages. He was not surprised; he had heard about this for several days, he had been desensitized to it. In his gut he felt sick, but he was all too familiar with what Tabbar and his forces were doing. He opened all the cages, freeing the children, and lining them up.

He led them up the staircase and up to where Tabbar's body was; they ignored it, giving it no notice.

Ali ascended the stairs, and found his mother's body lying on the floor, he ran towards her crying, hugging and kissing her, but she did not respond. Weeping quielty, he felt a hand delicatly touch his shoulder. It was Nahrayn. Ali looked at Nahrayn with sadness. Kneeling besides Sarah, Nahrayn placed her lips next to Sarah's ears, and for the first time in many months, she spoke.

"Wake up," whispered Nahrayn. The two children hugged and kissed their mother, they spoke to her, but still, Sarah did not respond.

"I won't let you leave so easily, not after all you've been through," said Alexander pulling Sarah's body and taking it upon his shoulder. He began to carry her body through the corridor as he led the children out.

"Don't worry," said Alexander to Ali and Nahrayn, "I will take care of her."

The children all followed Alexander as he hurried out of the underground prison. He was sprinting, and on his shoulder Sarah's body flailed, soaking Alexander's clothes in amber. When he had reached the entrance, the bright light of the sun blinded him. He could see the exit from where he stood. He walked towards the light, he left the darkness of the underground caverns. It had been a while since he had seen natural light, and so he found it refreshing to his mind.

Walking outside and feeling the fresh air dazzled him, and so he did not notice the bodies that lay on the floor. They were the bodies of two masked men, two of the terrorists. Against the wall in a bloody mess; sat the executioner. He knelt against the concrete wall; leaning against a large splatter of red, his own blood that had marked the wall behind him like paint upon a canvas. He sat smoking a cigarette, his rifle angled against the hot concrete.

"So, Tabbar... He was in the cellar?" asked the executioner taking a deep breath from his cigarette.

"You must leave, you must leave with us." said Alexander to the executioner.

"What I must do," said the executioner, "Is to set things right. My family, I lied about them, they are all dead. They were all killed a long time ago, killed before my eyes. I cannot go back to live a normal life, not after this." The executioner spoke, he looked at the children that accompanied Alexander, "Take them all with you, show them a new world."

In the distance several trucks were heading towards them. "I will take care of them while you escape, you have very little time, you must leave, now!"

The executioner readied another magazine of bullets, "They underestimated me, everyone underestimated, but now they won't," he whispered to himself, "Now things will be right, now I will find peace."

Alexander took the children. He ran away from the trucks. He ran through the desert, followed by the children and with Sarah on his shoulder. She weighed heavily on him. The Mesopotamian sun beat down harshly against his head, but he ran. Out of breath and thirsty, he could hear the children crying. The desert looked boundless, with no end in sight.

His feet were burning as he trod through the golden sand; the ground was hot, boiling with the ferocity of the sun. He fell to his knees. He looked at the children, they looked tired, thirsty and weak.

Don't worry, we're nearly there," said Alexander.

Rapid gunfire could be heard emanating from the hideout. That must have been the executioner, thought Alexander. The other terrorists must have seen what happened and killed the executioner for his betrayal.

Alexander got up once more, lifting Sarah with his aching body. The children surrounded him begging, at forty degrees celsius the thirst had struck them hard. They begged him for water, but he had none. He lied to them because that was all he could do, he told them that he knew where he was going, he told them that water was close; he told them to continue. But even he grew hopeless, he no longer knew if Sarah was alive. He considered leaving her body in the middle of the desert, but he quickly dropped the thought from his mind, and again took to running through the hot sand.

After an hour of traversing the desert, he fell to the floor realizing that his body could no longer take the weight and stress that it was put under. Sarah's body rolled off onto the sand. He looked at her in sadness, the children surrounded her. Ali grabbed hold of her and began to pull; Nahrayn saw Ali and joined him, soon all the children were pulling Sarah. They dragged her across the hot desert. Alexander took his shirt, and placed it under Sarah's body to cushion it from the hot sand.

Chapter 11

Worlds Of Darkness And Light

Tabbar stood in the darkness scared and alone. "Is anyone there?" he shouted into the nothingness, but nothing responded. Tabbar walked through these silent realms naked.

"If only you could see," echoed a voice in his mind. "If you were to see what I see, if you could feel what I feel..." The voice echoed once again.

"Who are you?"

"Dare not scream oh lost one," spoke the voice. He slowly began to see and discern two thin vertical lines. They monitored him, they followed him wherever he walked, and they were always close. He felt something lightly vibrate against his feet forcing him to jump back in fear. Sweat gushing from his forehead; he took deep and heavy breaths. He was floating within nothingness looking into the eyes of a demon.

"What you have sought, you never gained," spoke the strange creature to Tabbar, "What you have created for others, you have created for yourself; you defied me and the very creed that brought you here!"

"I was a God, people lived and died by my hands," responded Tabbar, "I took life, and I created life. There was no boundary that I would not cross, doing so, made me who I am, it made me excel beyond everyone else, and it made me limitless."

The monstrous eyes darted around him, looking like two red beams, in their path they created a trail of red. They quivered with anger, and inspected him menacingly from all angles.

"Then tell me, oh wise god..." spoke the eyes to him, "What do you have now? Create, if you are truly a God, create; and I shall bow down to you."

"What should I create?"

"Create whatever it is that you desire. Create a world of light, create beauty, create chaos if you must, create whatever your will desires." But Tabbar could not do any of those things, all he could do was look back at the eyes in fear.

"Just tell me, who are you? Do you know who I am!" shouted Tabbar at the eyes.

"I know you too well," spoke the demon, "But do you know yourself?" Tabbar looked away from the eyes, he was trying to run, trying to escape their gaze. "You are me, just as I am you. You are the bringer of destruction, pain and emptiness. Like you, I have become the bringer of those things," continued the demon.

Tabbar kept walking back, but the eyes followed him, ominously laughing. The demon was hissing at him. Falling to his back, Tabbar's fear had overwhelmed him and he had lost control of himself. Trying to get back to his feet, he struggled;

reaching to the floor he finds a lamp. Tabbar brings this lamp up to his face. It was a rusted lamp, it weighed heavily forcing him to strain his muscles. Within it he could see a small dark flame.

He reached out forward, stretching his arms before him, the lamp shaking with fear in his hands. He willed and prayed that the light within this lamp illuminate the darkness. But the flame did not grow, and it did not bear light.

"I will give you all that you want!" shouted Tabbar, "Whatever it is that you desire."

"But you have nothing, I am cold, and the darkness beckons to me, it calls me out," spoke the demon.

Sarah felt her soul take flight into different dimensions, planes and worlds. The illusion of the ego, the illusion of the self and those of the material world, all perished. Geometric patterns surrounded her; twirling, spiralling and shining. Strange beings greeted her as she passed through these worlds, many people did she see and meet.

She found herself landing into a paradise, the scent of flowers and honey entered her nostrils relaxing her. A luminous sun radiated this world of beauty. She saw colours that she did not know exist, all aspects of this new ineffable world. She hovered down to the ground, and when her feet did touch the ground, she saw the ground covered with beautiful, colourful radiant flowers. In the sky multicoloured birds soared, they sang soothing songs, gently easing her into this new world.

In front of her lay a colossal lamp that radiated splendidly, its warmth was peaceful, its beauty immeasurable. She had to cover her eyes and retract away from this lamp, for it was too bright. She felt as if she was being watched, she looked up at the sun with amazement, and saw two eyes watching her.

Something was up there, but she did not know what it was. Two warm loving eyes were looking down upon her, the great figure descended with a swift motion, landing before her silently. It was Azkazeal, he was bright, shining, like she had never seen before. He no longer looked like a Serpent, he seemed different. He was as infinite source of energy. He stretched his wings, spreading them to envelop her, they shone splendidly, and like two giant mirrors, they reflected the sunlight. Sarah saw that the sun he had descended from was the egg that he used to coil around. Upon his skin were beautiful markings, calligraphy that she had never seen before.

"Azkazeal is that you?" she asked.

The figure smiled back, and replied in the most beautiful of voices, "I welcome you, oh masterful one."

"What are those beautiful marks on your skin?" she asked.

"They are your actions oh Sarah," spoke Azkazeal, "The greatest of which; how you stretched your hand, giving help to those that need it. You not only saved people's lives, but you also saved their souls... But sadly, not all souls are capable of being saved.

"How do you mean?" she asked.

"Come with me," Azkazeal grabbed hold of Sarah dragging her into a world of complete darkness.

"Why have you brought me here, oh Azkazeal?"

"So that you may see the fate of the others."

In the distant darkness, she saw Tabbar, standing before a giant Serpent, as dark as the shadows. The Serpent's head was as big as Tabbar's body. Tabbar spoke to it in fear, falling to his knees pleading and begging for mercy, but the Serpent's laughs echoed through this dark realm.

"Is there no way to help him?" asked Sarah.

"No," replied Azkazeal, "Only he could have helped himself, but alas it is now too late."

Tabbar begged further from this strange Serpent, but it ignored him, poising itself in a striking position, it leapt with furious anger upon him, swallowing him whole. Tabbar entered the dark entity, engulfed in negativity. He felt a trembling and felt a strange aching in his soul. The faces of those he had met through his life were before him, apparitions coming and going. He screamed into the vile darkness for help, but nothing responded, except for the demons that he had created. The demons that awaited him were the demons that were hiding deep within his own psyche, the remnants of his actions and thoughts.

Azkazeal took Sarah to where Tabbar was. She looked on amazed by what she saw; Tabbar was inside this strange Serpent.

"Who is that serpent?" asked Sarah.

"He is Tabbar's guardian," replied Azkazeal.

A rhythmic vibration had taken over Tabbar's soul. The vibration kept increasing in tempo, like a flame with a voracious appetite it inhibited all his faculties. During which, mystical voices became discernible to Tabbar.

Tabbar came to find out that these were not merely voices, they weren't merely noises, they were a beautiful melody, all singing synchronized and harmoniously. This was the song of the universe, the voice of the cosmos, and the requiem of God!

He heard how all sang this song, all birds, trees and the stars. All sang in perfect unison, in harmony. Tabbar tried to speak to them, he tried to join, but he was voiceless. Each time he spoke, a hoarse voice echoed from his lips, and demons accompanied him. They were predatory looking beasts summoned from the deepest recesses of his mind. The world around him began to tighten and squeeze; he gasped for air.

A deep longing pain enamoured him, forcing him to scream, and the vibrations got stronger and stronger forcing his soul down further and further. For his soul was heavy from the suffering he had caused, and from the guilt he had carried. The last thing Sarah heard was Tabbar's scream as he descended into a world of oblivion.

"Do you see how he could not have been saved; he had descended too far into arrogance, into ignorance, and no longer was he worthy, his mission unfulfilled, and his memory long forgotten."

Azkazeal grabbed onto Sarah and pulled her back up through the dimensions back into her world of light.

"What will become of Tabbar?" asked Sarah as she took time to adjust to the light of her world.

"He will be judged, and so will the society that made him, there is no smoke without fire oh Sarah," replied Azkazeal. "Remember that power comes from many things, and in your world, power is money. But Sarah you defied that, you reached out to the world with your soul and not your possessions." Sarah was still mesmerised by Azkazeal's glow, she stared at it as he spoke, "If you had desired, you could have deceived yourself, but I am a part of you. Each time you thought in negativity, I grew darker and darker, my grip grew tighter and tighter, and the sun that now radiates this plane grew planer and planer. But, I am now purified, you have perfected yourself, and you have perfected me. And now, you have unified your heart and soul."

Chapter 12

Patience

The sphere above her radiated brighter than it had ever before. In this realm were beautiful colours and splendid plants. It was a beautiful scene, it quivered to the sound of an oasis that dripped from afar. Oceans could be seen, and she could smell the sweet scent of purified water. Her hair flailed in the saccharine winds. When she inspected her hair, she found it to be youthful. She touched her face, only to find the smoothest of skin, her hands as soft as snow. She thought of life, and it seemed so short, as if a blink of an eye. It was like a movie that had ended too quickly.

Alexander fell to the ground; in his arms were several children who had passed out. Behind him Sarah's body lay on the ground as Nahrayn and Ali wept over it, they hugged and tugged upon Sarah's body. They pleaded to the women that had inspired them. Alexander looked at all the children; he did not want to leave them to die alone. He knew that if he walked alone, if he wasn't forced to carry anyone that he could make it, he could walk much further. He questioned whether it would be best to leave them. He weighed the options, thinking that maybe if he could call for help, if he could make it on his own, that maybe he would be able to bring aid and save everyone. He took his time ruminating about all the possibilities. But he knew that he could never forgive himself if he ever left these children on their own.

He fell to the earth, recognizing the senselessness of what he was trying to achieve. There was no water and he could not see anyone in miles. He looked on into the distance noting how the heat gave the illusion of a swaying rippling effect of water; he was all too familiar with this mirage by now and ignored it. The children did not cry; they could not spare the energy.

"Help!" shouted Alexander into the distance. The children looked at him with concern, "Help!" he shouted once more, looking at the vultures that were now circling them, watching them. He walked over to Sarah's body inspecting it, looking through her pockets and garments. There he found a small mobile; it was the mobile that the translator had handed to her. Covered with blood and with a bullet lodged in it; it had stopped and deflected shards of metal from hitting her.

He then checked her wounds, made sure that the tightly wrapped pieces of clothe that he had used to stop her blood were still there. He checked Sarah's pulse and began to weep. Realizing that Ali and Nahrayn were watching him, he wiped away his tears and tried to regain composure.

Lying on the floor with the mobile in his hand, he had ran out of options, but there existed that small everpresent hope in his heart. Through the blood covered screen he could not make out anything, the cracked screen reflected fiercely against his eyes. He pressed random numbers on the mobile phone hoping that something may happen, but the phone made no noise, it did not respond. His hand fell to his side, and for a while he closed his eyes, waiting for death's embrace.

Suddenly, he heard crackling come from the phone, he brought it up to his face once more shouting in English, asking for help. He could not make out what was said or who was on the other line, but he shouted and pleaded.

The sun that radiated above Sarah began to descend, and she felt an urge to walk towards it. Voices in her head spoke to her, they told her, "Enter the light. Enter the world of eternity," so Sarah entered the sun that she had cultivated.

It felt like going through a tunnel, she could see a supreme ineffable truth at the end. As she passed through the tunnel she felt a warm energy and a love that she had never felt before. The vibrations increased like they had done with Tabbar. However the music that played to her was of her own journey, a tale eternally told through the ages within the requiem of God.

The rain of comfort and solitude was rippling atop her heart as she saw her husband waiting for her at the end. Then Azkazeal came, wrapping his body and wings around her with fury. He began pulling her, dragging her away from the light.

"Azkazeal! What are you doing?" she exclaimed.

"I will not let this happen, not now. I will fulfil my end!"

"No Azkazeal, let me go, they call me, the light, the beauty." she cried.

They struggled, Azkazeal dragging Sarah away from the light as she squirmed trying to escape his clutches. They passed through the vortex that beckoned to her, but Azkazeal exerted himself, pulling her away from the light. He pulled and tugged vehemently, with all his might and all his strength. The vortex was very powerful and he could not contain it for very long. She looked at the ineffable truth, mesmerized by it, like an insect attracted to a light. She saw her husband waiting for her, smiling.

"Patience Sarah, patience!" stammered Azkazeal, "Listen carefully."

"Let me go!" she screamed as she pushed Azkazeal away from her.

"Listen Sarah! Just listen!" thundered Azkazeal, his voice over taking the music of this vortex. So Sarah stopped, and she listened, she closed her eyes. And as she done so, she could hear faint voices; they whispered to her. They were familiar voices; they were the voices of Ali and Nahrayn.

"Come back, don't leave," they whispered, pleading and begging. Sarah looked away from the vortex, away from the light, and Azkazeal pulled her back.

"Bear with me, this is difficult and painful," said Azkazeal as he pulled her. So Azkazeal took hold of Sarah, and they both flew away from the light. Sarah looked at it, it was a beauty that was difficult to resist, but the voice of Ali, the voice of Nahrayn echoed in her heart sending sensations of joy through her body. She sought to be with them. She did not want to leave them alone, and she did not want them to live in a world void of love.

She felt her body being pulled; electric shocks swam through her; an indiscernible blissful energy. Azkazeal with all his might pushed once more forcing them out of the light, out of the vortex and back into her world. They flew out of the sun that she had cultivated. They sprang away from the sun, rocketing and landing into her world.

Azkazeal then quickly ascended to the skies, the sun rising with him. He grabbed hold of it, tightening his wings around it, preventing Sarah from entering.

"I shall guard it," he said as his wings dispersed the light of the sun through her world.

"As your guardian, I will only ever admit you, when the time has come to pass," said Azkazeal.

"Why did you stop me?" she asked "We could have both entered the light."

"Patience Sarah, I will now fulfil our oath, I will be waiting for you, but patience, just patience..." His voice resonated in her mind as he faded away. A light was blinding her.

"She's alive!" a voice shouted as she awoke. She was on a hospital operating table, the light in the operating room was beating into her eyes. It was very difficult for her to see who or what was happening around her. She felt a surge of blood rush through her skull, her head thumped with the beating of her heart. Slowly, the afterimage of Azkazeal began to fade, and she regained composure. Her head cooling, and her body filling with blood and life.

"It's a miracle!" one of the nurses squealed. The doctor had a look of complete shock upon his face, he looked at the defibrillator that he was holding, never had he seen someone brought back from death. When she was brought to the hospital, he had no hope, but he saw Ali and Nahrayn clinging onto Sarah. So he tried the impossible, he did not give up, and it had worked, she was brought back from death itself.

Her body ached, she was in pain. The painkillers may not have been enough, but she didn't need them. She saw the door to the room open, Ali and Nahrayn running towards her, crying, smiling. She embraced them, bringing them up to her beating heart. She remembered Azkazeal's voice, "patience" he echoed in her mind, "You are the flame that burns the wicked and warms the virtuous."

Sarah held Ali's head in her arms, she looked deep into his eyes, and began to cry. At that moment she felt happy, she felt at peace, a part of her soul had been restored. She kissed him on his forehead, in her heart she promised never to lose him again.

Alexander stood at the door, in his hand a camera. In his heart; a message, a story that he will never forget, one that he will tell the world. Alexander took the blood covered mobile from his pocket, he looked at it, and smiled.

Chapter 13

Apotheosis

So Sarah took her son back home, her new daughter with her too. She could remember her adventure. Her journey seemed almost unreal, but each night that she would sleep, she would meet Azkazeal, the guardian of the luminous gate. She did not tell anyone about Azkazeal or Mazaroth, for she knew that no one would believe her tale.

Alexander would travel the world, telling everyone of what he had experienced and seen. He had Tabbar's documents; they revealed the corruption that existed in the world. He would be the one to reach the masses through his writing, through his reports and documentaries. What had been a hidden world of corruption operating beneath the guise of governments and corporations, was now visible. Alexander offered to fly Sarah away from the madness.

The terrorist group that she had infiltrated were looking for her; they sought revenge for their comrades. Several terrorists organizations had placed a bounty on her. She was called a spy by the terrorists, a terrorist by the media, and a hero by her fellow man.

Amal's town was too dangerous to live in, and so Amal now lived with Nadda and her family. Sarah had taken Alexander up on his offer, she would travel the world to spread her message and the lessons that she had learnt. She would keep Ali and Nahrayn safe by leaving the chaos of Baghdad. And so she stood in the airport with her luggage. She was thinking about her uncle Raheem's words before she had come to the airport, "That wherever you may walk, your feet will find their place, your soul will find its destiny."

Ali and Nahrayn were running around and playing mirthfully. Nahrayn skipped between the airport seats, and Ali was spinning and whirling till he got dizzy; Sarah saw them and smiled. Amal and Nadda stood before her, they were proud of their friend. They would miss her, but they knew that she had a new goal; she must travel the world spreading her message. They knew that she was no longer voiceless.

"When you first told me, that you would try and change the world, I never really believed that you would," said Nadda, "I thought you would give up, I thought you would come back home."

Sarah felt sad that she had to leave her home, but she knew that her circumstances called for it.

"I will come back," said Sarah, "I will not be gone forever."

"No, we need you there," said Nadda, "You are now our voice, you are now our hope."

"Will we still talk of the past? Of how we played as kids, of how we chased the moon?" asked Sarah smiling.

"No my dear friend, all we will talk about, is how one woman, can change the world," said Nadda smiling back,

"Amal," said Sarah, "You gave me hope when I felt lost, your cheerful smile was there when I most needed it, if you ever need anything, you can always call, and I will be there." To this Amal did not respond, she wiped the tears away from her eyes, and gave Sarah a nod of acknowledgement. The three friends had spent many days talking amongst each other. They thought that it would be easy to say goodbye, but as they stood there, they realized that they did not know for how long Sarah would be gone. And so they felt a deep sadness. But for them, there was nothing that was needed to be said, for they knew that deep in their hearts, there was an unbreakable bond. Amal and Nadda embraced Sarah, they hugged her tightly, they kissed Ali and Nahrayn, waving goodbye to them, and saw their friend off onto the plane.

She chose her seat on the aircraft and placed her luggage into the compartments above. Ali and Nahrayn sat next to the window; they stared outside in awe as they saw the world shrink before them.

Sarah was to go and meet Alexander, he had organized an interview with her on TV. When the plane had taken off, and the passengers had time to adjust, Sarah fell into a deep slumber. Her head resting against the headrest. Before her stood Azkazeal.

"I need to show you something," said the figure of light, "Look behind you, and look into the distance."

So Sarah began to stare into the distance behind her, and as she did, the indiscernible became discernible, and she could see. There stood Alexander, Mazaroth bowing before him.